VALOR
IN
THE DARKNESS

J. A. GUINN

HEMINGWAY
PUBLISHERS

TABLE OF CONTENTS

CHAPTER 1

The heavy-duty, corrugated cardboard box that once held a large refrigerator or freezer now wrapped around me, weighing me down like a soggy, tomb-like blanket from the heavy rainstorm earlier in the evening. Despite wearing multiple layers—including long underwear, ragged Levi's, water-resistant (keyword: resistant) rain pants, two sweatshirts, and an insulated Carhartt jacket—I was still soaked to the skin. On a typical night, I might expect four to five hours of sleep before hunger pangs woke me, tempting me to rummage through the dumpster a block down the alley for something to eat. Tonight, my body was trembling from the dropping temperatures and the relentless rain, and I hadn't slept a single wink. I knew that if I didn't pull myself together and find something to do, I probably wouldn't see the dawn of a new day.

Although I very briefly considered just remaining in my cardboard tomb and allowing the cold and damp to claim my body, something inside, something in my heart, told me to move, to pull myself up by my bootstraps. That was something my father would tell me.

My father, a veteran of the Korean War and Vietnam conflict, was a pillar of strength. His words, even in his absence, guided my actions. "Joshua Griggs! Get up! Make something of yourself! There are no slackers in this family!" His voice was a constant reminder of the resilience I inherited from him, which kept me going even in the darkest of nights.

My father returned from Vietnam physically crippled but mentally as alert and active as any twenty-year-old. The Medal of Honor they had hung around his neck on his return from Nam lay buried in a drawer with his other medals. He didn't talk much about it because he didn't feel worthy of the honor.

Finally, with his words drilled into my head, I forced myself up and struggled out of the soggy box's constraints onto my feet. I tucked my hands inside my jacket beneath my armpits for whatever little warmth remained in my body. Leaning against the brick wall behind me for support, my body felt like a Raggedy Ann doll with most of the stuffing missing. My soaked, shapeless Western Stetson, which had seen better days, funneled the rain down to the front of the brim, where it ran off in rivulets. At that moment, I was not a homeless man but a vulnerable human being struggling to survive.

My body continued to quiver from the cold and damp, as I hunched my shoulders against the still-falling rain and slowly shuffled down the alley to the nearest dumpster. Nothing there. I was too late. Several blocks away was another dumpster I had only visited once, but it was now the closest one with any hope of finding something to eat, as it was also located behind a restaurant. I wasn't sure I could make it that far, but that was my only reasonable option. The previous day had yielded little nourishment.

After I saw that my usual dumpsters had already been gone through by other homeless people late at night, I realized that anything discarded by the restaurant earlier in the evening had probably already been examined by others like me. The chance of finding anything edible was slim, but I had to try.

Stopping to rest every block, I finally made it to the dumpster, and within minutes of rummaging through its trash debris, I discovered that I was right; nothing was salvageable, at least nothing I could stomach. As I slumped against the dumpster, trying to decide my next move, a door squeaked open, and a brilliant shaft of light lanced through the dark alley, causing me to raise my hand to shield my squinted eyes from the piercing light.

A slight squeal of surprise from the doorway startled me. Quickly turning my back to the light and what I expected to be a demeaning outburst meant to chase me away, I started to limp back down the alley. But after only two steps, what I heard instead, above the clatter of rain on the metal rooftops of the buildings on each side of the alley, stopped me dead in my tracks.

"Wait! Don't go! Are you hungry? I can get you something to eat."

This was the first time such an incident had happened. Usually, business owners chased my kind away because they believed loitering vagrants would harm their businesses. Things had been thrown at me, and I had even been sprayed with a hose sometimes to make me leave a restaurant. I had not met anyone from this restaurant before, so this kind gesture stopped me.

Slowly turning around with my arms crossed in front of me in a protective mode and with my shoulders hunched up against the cold, I thought maybe I had died and gone to heaven, although I did not believe heaven was where I belonged.

The person standing silhouetted fifteen feet in front of me seemed to glow in the dark, with a halo of light around her. I couldn't see many details, except for a smile that stretched from ear to ear and hair piled on top of her head. I felt frozen in place. Was this person luring me in so I could be chastised, or were the comments I heard as caring and empathetic as they seemed?

"Please come back. I didn't mean to startle you. I was just surprised. You can warm up, and I'll fix something for you to eat. Please. I won't hurt you."

She didn't realize I was the one who usually caused the pain because she didn't know me.

What choice did I have? With no idea where I would get my next piece of food, let alone a whole meal, this woman showed me a kindness I hadn't felt in a long time. Shuffling, one step at a time, I painfully limped toward the shaft of light and the welcoming woman's outstretched hand. I suspected that once I got close enough to her, my stench would drive her back into the restaurant, and she would slam the door in my face, but that didn't happen. Instead, she welcomed me with open arms, and for the first time in a long time, I felt a glimmer of hope and gratitude.

In past months, as a Marine on active duty, I had been skilled at recognizing and understanding people's expressions and body language, which saved my life more than once in Afghanistan. What I now saw on this angel's face as I approached her was a song of empathy, sincerity, and caring. Cautiously, I allowed her to take my elbow and guide me through the door into the restaurant's kitchen. Surprisingly, she did not seem repulsed by me. After closing the door behind us, she slipped past me, grabbed a chair from a corner, and placed it next to a table that looked like it was used for cutting vegetables, as various remnants remained there.

"Sit here." She helped lower me into the chair. "I'll be right back."

Wearily settling myself into the chair, water dripped onto the floor from the front of my Stetson. Pulling it off and removing the scarf wrapped around my head and neck, I ran one hand through my long, unkempt hair, attempting to look a little decent, but I knew it was a failed attempt. Nothing was decent about my appearance. Besides my mop of hair, my face was sheathed with several months of dark, black beard in about the same shape as my hair.

Within seconds, this little angel, who could only be five feet three inches tall and a hundred pounds soaking wet, returned with a small space heater. She plugged the heater into a wall outlet and set it before me. The heater's glow enveloped me with a physical and emotional warmth that penetrated my core. My gloves were wet and threadbare, so I pulled them off, stuffing them into a jacket pocket, knowing I would need them later, and I didn't want to lose them.

Curiously, I watched this woman at another table as she loaded various food items onto a plate, then placed it into a large microwave oven. While the microwave hummed, she took a large mug from an overhead cabinet, filled it with coffee, and brought it to me. Strands of blond hair that had escaped from her bun danced around her face. She moved through the kitchen with the grace of an athlete and the confidence of someone who knew her purpose in life.

She handed me the mug of coffee. "Do you want cream and sugar?"

I had not spoken to her until then, but now I had to respond. "No. Thanks."

Hesitantly, I took the hot mug in my hands, enjoying its warmth. The microwave's ding signaled that the food was ready. Carefully removing the plate with a hot pad, she approached and set the food on the table, along with a knife and fork.

"My name is Marcie. What's your name, if I may ask?"

I was about to put my fork into what appeared to be a piece of meatloaf, but stopped when she asked my name. I looked up into her angelic face. "Joshua. My name is Joshua."

"Nice to meet you, Joshua. I have some other clean-up to do in the restaurant, so you go ahead and eat. There's plenty of coffee, so holler when you want more."

"Thank you." I was able to mumble. After she turned to pick up a mop, and as I prepared to put the first bite into my mouth, I stopped as I remembered to make the sign of the cross before I ate. I didn't often pray before eating, as most of the time I could only find food remnants in dumpsters. But this was an authentic meal, and the Lord deserved my thanks. Then, since I noticed Marcie had her back to me, I dove into the food, not paying much attention to my manners.

I was starving, and it was tough to control my eating. When she came back, I had already finished the meal, licking the plate clean and draining my coffee mug.

Although I suspected the answer in advance, I still needed to say, "I'm sorry, ma'am. I can't pay you for this."

"Oh. No. Not at all expected," she responded to me. "But I do have one request."

Oh, oh. She will probably ask me never to come back here again, I thought to myself. Standing with my hat in my hand, I said, "Don't worry, ma'am, I won't bother you again. Thank you so much for your kindness tonight." I turned to walk toward the alley door.

"What? Wait! I wasn't going to tell you not to come back. I was going to say that when you're in need, please don't hesitate to come back! I usually close the restaurant this time of night and always have leftovers, so whenever you come back while I'm still here, I'll have something for you. Okay? Promise me you will do that?"

"That is very kind of you, ma'am. I appreciate that, but I don't want to bother you or get you in trouble with your boss."

"That would be hard since I am the boss," she declared with a beaming smile. "So, you can just come by whenever you want."

"Thanks again." I put my still-wet hat back on, tightened it, and headed for the alley door. Just as I was about to step into the alley, I heard a crackling noise of breaking glass coming from the front of the restaurant. Looking over my shoulder, I saw Marcie walking back into the restaurant. Hesitating for a moment with my hand on the alley door handle, I heard a scream.

Limping back into the kitchen but forgetting to close the alley door behind me, I saw a broom leaning against a wall. I picked it up and struck it against my good knee, breaking off the straw part and leaving a four-foot handle. Holding the broom handle by my side, I cautiously moved into the restaurant dining area. Even though the lights were dim, I could tell some kind of struggle was happening, so I paused to assess the scene.

It took me only seconds to understand the situation. Three street thugs—two of whom I believed to be tormentors of homeless people, stealing food or valuables after knocking their victims senseless— were attacking Marcie. Most of the homeless weren't in any condition to fight back, but Marcie was putting up a good fight. As a Marine, I had always been able to show enough resistance to keep such attackers at bay. Of course, my six-foot-four-inch height and former 220-pound weight usually helped me fend off most thugs. Now, however, I was just lucky enough to be able to move around, searching for food or shelter.

The scuffle I observed in front of me sparked my temper, sending an adrenaline rush through my body and giving me the strength and energy I had not experienced in a long time. Two of the ruffians had hold of Marcie, one of whom was ripping at her blouse. The third man was attempting to open the cash register at the front counter. Fortunately, they all had their backs to me.

Although I stood as tall as I could, the limp in my right leg from a shrapnel wound sustained during an ambush in Afghanistan might suggest to these guys that I was weak and vulnerable. Hoping that my size would intimidate them, I moved further into the restaurant with the most commanding, gruffest voice I could muster. "I don't think this lady wants all that much attention, guys. Leave her alone and go crawl back into the sewer!"

All activity stopped, and silence permeated the room as the three turned toward me in unison with surprised looks. They appeared unused to being confronted or challenged, especially by someone like me. Then, with sneers and grins of confidence—actually overconfidence—on their faces, knowing they outnumbered me, they gave me their full attention. The apparent leader, who had been ripping Marcie's blouse, pulled out a knife, the six-inch blade popping out as he pushed a button on the side, pointing it at me. "You'd better leave and return to whatever trash heap you crawled out of, dude. This is none of your business."

I reprimanded them again, this time with venom in my voice. "You little dirtbags need to leave! Now! Using a woman to protect you from garbage like me demonstrates how cowardly you are." I prayed this comment would cause them to push Marcie out of the way, where she would no longer be at risk of injury from what I was about to do to these thugs.

"We don't need her for protection against you. We can beat your sorry ass into the ground with ease." With that, the apparent leader pushed Marcie into one of the booths, and as the other two also pulled knives, they started edging toward me. The leader was coming straight at me with the other two, one going to my left and one to my right, working around tables in their way.

As they approached, I balanced on the balls of my feet, assessing the three men and trying not to favor my injured leg. The greasy-haired leader was just under six feet tall with a large stomach, so he wouldn't be moving quickly. His hair was tied back in a ponytail, and he had a scruffy beard and mustache. The dark-skinned, emaciated-looking punk moved to my left. His face was covered with sores, and he seemed to be a meth addict. I had seen plenty of addicts on the streets over the past few months. This punk's body appeared to jerk constantly. He kept tossing his knife from one hand to the other—an amateur move. The third man, I believed, was the one I should fear most. He was a muscular Hispanic man who handled his knife with confidence.

I had switched the broom handle to my left hand when I entered the dining area from the kitchen, but I still kept it hidden behind my leg. With the dim restaurant lighting, I believed it went unnoticed by the three thugs. Using a body motion I hoped would suggest I was going after the skinny guy on my left first, I watched the Hispanic on my right move into my seemingly unprotected side with confidence. Just before the Hispanic reached me, I swung the broom handle out from behind my leg with all the agility I could muster, hitting my attacker's hand at the wrist. A crack like a broken branch echoed as the broomstick struck, causing the knife to fall to the floor, breaking the broomstick in half, and making the Hispanic scream a profanity as he dropped to the floor, cradling his arm.

Not wasting more time on this attacker, who was temporarily down, I lunged back at the meth addict, jabbing the end of the broomstick into his throat. By then, the apparent leader had stopped moving forward, realizing he might have bitten off more than he could chew. He turned back toward the booth where he had pushed Marcie and grabbed her by the arm, but before he could turn around, I hurled the remnants of my broomstick like a boomerang at the attacker, hitting him in the back of the neck. The leader collapsed to the floor in a heap, bouncing against the booth where Marcie had huddled.

The only sounds left in the room were the labored breathing of the meth addict with his hands clutched to his throat, blood leaking out between his fingers, and the moans of the Hispanic with the broken wrist. As Marcie started to extricate herself from the booth, stepping over the collapsed leader on the floor, she suddenly screamed and pointed behind me. I turned, but before I could raise an arm in defense, I felt a blow to the side of my head that knocked me to the floor. My ears rang, but I knew I had to get into a defensive position if I didn't want to end up in the morgue. Turning on my side, curling into a ball to protect my vitals, I saw, then felt a boot catch me in the side, forcing all the air out of my lungs. I suspected the next target would be my head, and if I took a severe blow there, it would be lights out for me.

Instinctively, as I covered my face with my hands for protection, I saw between my fingers a black boot pulled back, ready for another kick. I closed my eyes, waiting for the impact, hoping my hands would shield my head somewhat. The blow never landed. A crashing sound of broken wood echoed through the small restaurant, and then a body collapsed on the floor just inches from my face. When I looked up, I saw Marcie standing beside me, holding the remnants of one of the restaurant chairs. The remaining parts of the chair were scattered across the floor and on top of the surprise attacker, who had apparently entered the restaurant through the unlocked alley door.

Marcie stepped over the inert body on the floor, and even with her blouse torn, exposing her black lacy bra, she reached down to help me up off the floor. "Are you all right? Let's get you into a chair so I can look at you."

As I teetered to steady myself on a chair, my damaged senses lit up with flashing red and blue lights. The cops were here. I had to leave. Gently, I eased Marcie's hands off my arm, struggled to get out of the chair, and headed for the back door amid Marcie's protests.

"I have to go. I can't be here."

"No, it'll be okay. I'll report the incident to the police. It was not your fault."

"No, I can't." I grabbed my hat from the table in the kitchen and limped out the alley door as fast as my legs would permit, holding my side in pain, thinking I probably had a couple of broken ribs. Even though my stomach was full and I had warmed up considerably, I still needed shelter from the ongoing rain. I needed a place and time to recover.

CHAPTER 2

"Ma'am, are you trying to tell me that you are responsible for this mayhem? You took out all four of these individuals by yourself? I find that hard to believe," the thirty-year-old police officer questioned Marcie with obvious doubt in his voice, which also registered on his face, as evidenced by raised eyebrows.

"Yes, sir. I did. They broke in trying to rob me and attacked me, as you can see by my torn blouse." Marcie was holding her blouse together with one hand to prevent exposing herself to these officers. A second officer was placing the four attackers into restraints. As she said this, the Hispanic male on the floor with the broken wrist raised his head, spitting out, "No, she did…" but before he could complete what he was going to say, Marcie aimed a kick at his injured hand, causing him to scream in pain again as her foot impacted his wrist.

"Shut up, you imbecile!" She turned back to the police officer, standing as tall as she could at only five feet four inches, and said, "Please follow me, officer." Marcie strode over to a wall at one end of the restaurant. Flipping on an overhead light, she pointed to framed photographs on the wall and spoke with a slight reprimand in her voice. "See those pictures? Recognize anyone in them?" Then, seeing the confusion in the officers' eyes, she continued without giving him a chance to respond. "That's me in those three photos. I'm the one in the desert combat gear, wearing the helmet with an eighty-pound pack on my back and the rifle across my chest. I served two tours in Afghanistan with the U.S. Marine Corps. Now, do you doubt I can take care of myself?" she spat out as she stood just inches from the officer, looking up at his face with her hands on her hips in a defiant pose.

Holding his hands defensively, the officer took a few steps back, saying, "Okay. Okay. I believe you. Don't bite my head off."

"Well, I've got cleaning up to do, so if you two"—as she pointed to the other officer—"are finished here, would you take this scum with you as you leave? It is late, and I need to be open early tomorrow."

"Yes, ma'am. We'll get out of your hair."

Two ambulances had arrived, and the EMTs waited outside the restaurant until law enforcement cleared the scene of any hazards. They now entered at the direction of the officers, packaged up the injured attackers, and moved them out into the waiting ambulances.

As the two officers exited the restaurant, the officer with whom she had the confrontation turned to her and said, "If you need anything or decide you have any additional information to add, please call us."

"Thank you, officer." Then, reentering her kitchen, she retrieved an unbroken broom and a dustpan from a utility closet and cleaned up the broken glass and pieces of the shattered chair off the floor. She still needed to find a way to secure the broken pane of glass in the front door, but she had the necessary tools and some scrap wood in another storage closet. There was bound to be something there she could use to temporarily cover the hole until she could call someone for the repair. It was still going to be midnight before she finished closing up for the night. *I wonder who that homeless man was,* she thought as she worked. *It seemed like he didn't want to have any contact with the police, so maybe he was wanted by them. It just didn't seem right to drag him into this whole mess. He appeared to have enough problems of his own.*

Despite her Marine Corps training, she knew she couldn't have fought off those thugs alone. They would have drained her cash register of the day's proceeds, and only God knows what they might have done to her. Some rather unsavory characters had visited her restaurant, but generally, they behaved themselves. Rarely did any customer order a meal, eat, and leave without paying or causing a disturbance. This was the first time anything this violent had happened, and Marcie wondered if a new gang of some sort had moved into the neighborhood. She couldn't recall seeing any of these four there for a meal.

She chose this area to open her restaurant using the insurance money she received after her husband's death. They had met in Afghanistan and married during a leave in the United States. She requested a stateside assignment since she had already completed two tours in Afghanistan. She was told that because of the image she projected, she was a poster child for recruiting female Marines, so she was assigned to a recruiting station in Bellevue, Washington. Three months later, her husband was killed by an IED in Afghanistan. His death left a deep hole in her heart, even though they had only known each other for a year and hadn't been together long enough to have children. Moping around for several months didn't help until her mother convinced her to use the insurance money for something meaningful.

After conducting thorough research, she donated a significant portion of the money to Tunnels2Towers. In this charity, the CEO was a volunteer who received no pay, unlike Wounded Warriors, where the CEO earned an annual salary of over $350,000. She wanted to see tangible results from her giving and to know that most of her donation went directly to those in need, which, from her understanding, didn't always happen with the Wounded Warrior Project. Her mother had been a great cook; Marcie had learned a lot from her while growing up. When she got the idea to open a budget-friendly restaurant, as she called it, to serve good food at low prices for those who couldn't afford to eat at more expensive places, she began looking for an affordable building in a low-rent area. Her current location had been a failed restaurant, partly because they charged too much. The building didn't require much remodeling, just removing all the fancy fixtures to make it look more like a typical mom-and-pop spot.

From the beginning, she was overloaded with customers, often families to whom she gave discounts. Her mother had been an enormous help in getting started, doing a lot of the cooking and some of the bookkeeping. Although the restaurant was small, with only ten tables, she wanted to provide some room to move between them. She secured a two-for-one deal by hiring her sister as a part-time cook and waitress.

Even with all her customers, she barely broke even after paying expenses most months. Of course, her mother would not accept any money from her. However, with the savings she accumulated from her military service, her husband's insurance, and the Survivor Benefit Plan, which provided about 55% of her husband's military pay, she was still able to live comfortably. Her goal was not to become wealthy but to support the community, which gave her a satisfaction money couldn't match.

Finally, after sweeping up all the debris, she found a piece of plywood, some screws, and a drill, and began covering the broken window. Part of her job in the Marine Corps was vehicle maintenance, so she knew her way around a toolbox. Satisfied with her repair job, she looked at the clock and saw it was just past midnight. She decided it was time to go home. She usually opened for breakfast by seven or seven-thirty, which made for very long days, and staying busy helped her keep her mind off the recent loss of her husband.

With her purse over her shoulder and one hand inside it, gripping a can of pepper spray, Marcie cautiously stepped out the front door, looking up and down for any threats. She usually did this out of habit, especially tonight after the altercation. No one was loitering that she could see, including the man who had helped her. Remembering his name was Joshua, she recalled that he certainly knew how to handle himself, despite his appearance as a homeless person. He was probably a former military member, like her. She hoped he would take her up on her offer to return for meals if needed. Any chance to thank him properly for his help had escaped when he limped out the door upon the police's arrival. She wondered if his leg had been injured in the altercation… but now it was time to head home.

Marcie lived with her mother. Her sister had her own family with one child just three blocks away, and her brother had his own apartment. Even with those three family members, whom she frequently saw, she still experienced bouts of loneliness. Although it had only been six months since she lost her husband, she missed that kind of companionship, but the restaurant kept her too busy to form a relationship with anyone. She had gotten to know most of her customers reasonably well, especially those who regularly came for meals, but no one had caught her attention. That wasn't to say she cared to get to know Joshua better, but he had possibly saved her life. He certainly had saved the several hundred dollars in the till from those thugs. That alone was enough to warrant her showing him extra kindness if she ever saw him again.

****

Even though the rain and wind had lessened, I was still drenched from the incident at the restaurant. No longer hungry, I still needed to find shelter for the night as I walked down the dark street. Most of the streetlights in this area had been vandalized, but the security lights from the few remaining businesses offered a little illumination through their front windows.

Four blocks later, I stealthily entered a four-level parking garage that adjoined a large apartment complex. It was right on the edge of where I usually hung out. I was aware of several homeless shelters in this part of town, but I had been kicked out of them for unacceptable behavior, as the managers called it. But I could not abide disrespect and abuse of women or children, not by the staff of these shelters, but by other homeless men who thought they could take advantage of unaccompanied small families.

I usually didn't throw the first punch, but I responded in self-defense, sometimes too forcefully, which would get me ejected. A strong sense of right and wrong was a big part of my personality, but I often got punished for it. Sometimes, people resisted the existence of God, saying, "How could there be a God with all the evil in the world?" But I believed that without God, there would be no right and wrong, no good or evil. There would only be "I do what I want" or "I do what works."

Now, trying not to do anything wrong, it was still a matter of finding a dry, or better yet, a warm shelter for the night. Moving carefully along the row of parked cars, I kept an eye out for security guards who patrolled these garages. I occasionally tried door handles, hoping to find one unlocked. I knew I risked setting off a car alarm on every vehicle I touched, but I was willing to take that chance. When I rounded a corner and headed up to the next level, I heard a car door open and saw an interior dome light turn on and then off as someone exited a vehicle and shut the door.

Hiding behind a concrete pillar, I watched the occupant standing in front of his car, repeatedly pressing the key fob to activate the alarm after he closed the door, but it seemed futile. Finally, with a string of profanity, the man shoved his keys into his pocket and headed toward a nearby elevator. After the elevator doors closed, I slowly moved toward the car and tried the back door. It opened. The young owner was so accustomed to using a remote key fob that he forgot he could manually lock the door and use the key to unlock it in the morning. It's remarkable how many people have come to rely on technology instead of traditional methods.

The car was a large Lincoln Continental with a spacious back seat. Climbing in and shutting the door behind me, I could already feel the residual heat from the vehicle seeping into my wet clothes. My dark clothing blended well with the dark leather upholstery of the back seat. I hoped to get several hours of restful sleep. Anything would be better than the last couple of days spent out in the cold and rain with only a cardboard box for shelter. With thoughts of the angel, Marcie, whom I had met earlier that evening, I quickly drifted off to sleep.

CHAPTER 3

When Marcie returned to her restaurant the next day at 6:00 a.m., her mother, Maxine, was already working in the kitchen. Because she returned home late the night before, her mom had already gone to bed, and Marcie went straight to sleep without talking about the restaurant incident. As Marcie walked through the front door toward her mom, Maxine left the kitchen and approached her, her hands on her hips, and a worried look on her face.

"What's with the broken window, my dear? Did something happen last night that I should know about?"

This response from her mother was not unexpected, so Marcie plopped herself down in a chair by one of the tables, let out a big sigh, and then looked up at her mom, who was still standing in front of her with her hands on her hips. "It was just a minor incident, Mom. Someone tried to break in last night while I was cleaning up and preparing to leave. The intrusion alarm triggered an alert, and the police responded and took them away. Not much to it." Her mom always worried about her, so Marcie did not want to give her any more details than necessary.

"Did they get anything? The money in the till?"

"No, nothing, and I did this patch job until I could call to get the window repaired. I'll do that as soon as the shops open." With that, she pulled out her cell phone and searched for the repairman's number she had previously used. She would call him later.

"Let's get to work, Mom. You know Friday mornings are our busiest times," Marcie stated as she walked past her mom into the kitchen to retrieve an apron from the hook by the small walk-in freezer. As she opened the freezer door, she saw something dark on the floor under the table where she had fed Joshua the previous night. It was a scarf that he abandoned when he rushed out.

Marcie's mother had been watching her daughter, suspecting there was something she wasn't sharing about the previous night. Now, she saw Marcie glance at the table, so she turned and walked over to her. Reaching under the table, she pulled out the still-wet, dripping wool scarf. She held it up to Marcie and asked, "What is this? Where did this come from? It doesn't look like yours." She then placed her face close to the scarf and wrinkled her nose. "This smells like it has been wrapped around a dirty, wet dog."

Caught, she thought. She might as well be honest with her mom, or at least share most of the truth. "Okay, so don't be upset, Mom. I know you've told me more times than I can count to be careful around people experiencing homelessness, that many are on drugs, and some are violent." She paused and saw that her mom wouldn't let her off the hook easily. "Well, last night, while emptying the trash, I saw a homeless man going through the dumpster looking for food, so I brought him inside and made him a meal from leftovers. When those punks broke in, he helped me fight them off, but he ran off when the police arrived. He was in such a hurry that he forgot his scarf, which he probably needed."

"Okay, I won't tell you 'I told you so' since he seemed to help you, but you know how risky it is just to have a restaurant in this area, let alone letting strangers in the back door when you're alone. Please don't do that again. All right?"

"Mom, you know I'm careful. I had my pepper spray, but if it hadn't been for Joshua, who knows what would have happened to me, and the till would've been emptied for sure."

"Joshua!" her mother exclaimed, "How well do you know this guy?"

"Last night was the first time, and I asked him his name. He was very polite. I had nothing to fear from him. I offered him a meal whenever he needed one so he could return."

"Oh, for heaven's sake, young lady! Haven't I taught you anything?"

"Yes, mother, you have mostly talked about how to help others in need and share what I have. That's what I'm doing and what you have taught me. We have work to do now, so let's get off this topic and get breakfast ready."

Maxine finally relented, smiled at her daughter's compliments, and convinced herself that Marcie was right and she worried too much about her daughter. Marcie could take care of herself. Walking up behind her, Maxine wrapped her arms around her daughter, thanked her, and kissed her on the back of her head. Maxine then grabbed a dozen eggs from the fridge to make some omelets.

By 10:00 a.m., the breakfast crowd had thinned, giving Marcie and her mom a chance to sit with their coffee. As they discussed their lunch plans for that day, the bell on the front door jingled, and Marcie saw the confrontational police officer from the previous night walk in. She could tell the officer's presence made the few remaining patrons nervous, so she stood up and walked over to him at the front of the restaurant.

"Good morning, Officer Duncan." She had not learned his name from the previous night, but she now saw the obvious name tag attached to the right pocket of his uniform. "What can I do for you this morning? Are you here for breakfast?"

"Afraid not, ma'am. I wanted to let you know that those individuals who attacked you last night are already out of the hospital and out of our jail on bail. A lawyer came in this morning and posted their bond. They did not look happy, so I thought it prudent to warn you—they might be back to cause you trouble."

"That's too bad," Marcie said calmly, though she didn't feel it. "I suspect I will have to testify if I want them punished for what they did. Otherwise, they'll go free."

"That's correct, and they likely won't look at your testimony very favorably, so you need to watch yourself. I would suggest you never stay here alone late at night. We can have a car patrol pass by several times during the night until their trial, if they don't jump bail and disappear."

"Thank you for the suggestion. Now that I know what to expect, I'll stay alert and be prepared. Is there anything else?"

"Well, I was wondering…" Officer Duncan then moved closer to Marcie, lowering his voice. "Would you be interested in having dinner with me sometime?"

Raising her left hand, which still held her wedding ring, she emphatically said, "Sorry, but I'm married."

"Oh, sorry, I've never seen your husband around when I've been driving past here."

Marcie looked at him until she finally said, "I have work to do. Thanks for coming by." Turning around, she went back to the table to finish her coffee with her mom. She heard the doorbell jingle as Officer Duncan left the restaurant.

"What was that all about?"

"Mom, he was just informing me of the status of the punks from last night. They're already bailed out of jail by a lawyer this morning. He also asked me out."

"You don't look very excited about being asked out. He was a good-looking young man, and sometimes, you need some relaxing time away from work."

"Well, not him! His behavior last night indicated he didn't think a woman could take care of herself. I don't need to be hanging around someone like that."

With their coffee finished and her mom no longer commenting on Marcie's social life, they returned to the kitchen to prepare for the lunch customers. Lunch was usually quieter than breakfast, so there wasn't much to do.

****

With the sun piercing through the remaining rain clouds from the previous night's storm waking me up, I knew I needed to get out of this car before the owner came back. Luckily, the security guard patrolling the lot didn't find me during the night. I should remember this spot, though it was unlikely I would find this car unlocked again.

Even though it was cold, the bright morning sun lifted my spirits. I'd had a good night's sleep and a solid meal the night before, and I was relatively warm and dry. Leaving the parking garage and walking along the sidewalk, I passed several makeshift shelters used by other homeless people, like me. Turning into an alley known to have dumpsters that often held decent food scraps, I nearly bumped into one of my friends.

"Rafe, hey there, buddy, how ya doin'?"

Rafe was also a Marine who had been medically discharged due to his duty injuries in Afghanistan, but unlike me, Rafe's injuries had left him in a wheelchair. Rafe did not experience the PTSD symptoms that I had, but his support system had also failed him, which resulted in him being out on the street. He, however, had been able to maintain his calm, and he could find shelter and food at various warming shelters.

"Doin' good, guy. How about you?"

"Not bad. Believe it or not, I had a good meal in a restaurant last night. Then, I found a warm car to sleep in. Feeling pretty good today."

"Have you had anything to eat yet this morning, Joshua?"

"No. I just headed out to do that. Why?"

"Well, I just happened to have acquired a little extra at breakfast this morning, and I thought you might be able to use it for all you have done for me over the months." Pulling out a paper sack, Rafe produced sausage, two hard-boiled eggs, two apples, and a squished banana.

"Wow. That's great, Rafe. I don't need all of that, but the sausage, an egg, and an apple would be perfect."

"You got it, man," Rafe said as he handed the items to me.

Sitting on a trash can in the alley while I ate, I turned to Rafe. "Hey, do you remember those guys who have hassled everyone up and down the street the last few weeks? The ones that tipped you over in your wheelchair?"

"How could I forget them? I haven't seen them in a couple of days, though. Why do you ask?"

"I ran into them at that restaurant where I had dinner last night. They were bothering the owner. My temper got the best of me, so I took them down. Well, I took down three of them. A fourth one snuck up behind me and hit me hard on the head. He was about to kick me into the next state when the owner grabbed a chair and knocked him to the ground. The police took them away, but I managed to slip out. You know I can't let the police see me."

"Yeah, I know. Well, thanks for taking them off the street. Maybe we'll have some peace and quiet for a while."

"Let's hope they stay in jail for a while. I'm a little afraid that if they get out, they'll go back to harass that little angel."

"A little angel. Maybe you should go back there to check on her and get yourself another meal, my friend. Invite me along sometime, too," Rafe said with a twinkle in his eye, hinting at a deeper meaning behind his words.

"I would do that, but she isn't going to give either of us a second look. Anyway, thanks for the breakfast, Rafe. I need to find a place to stay tonight. Oh, and by the way, have you seen Wolf lately? I haven't seen him in a couple of days."

"He had to have some more surgery on his shoulder. I expect that we'll see him back here in a day or two."

"Wow. How was he going to pay for that?"

"Don't know. I heard a vets' group was going to cover part of it. The VA covers the rest, I think."

"Okay. Let me know if you hear he's having trouble handling it. I know he doesn't like hand-outs, but I may still have some money saved and can provide him with some of it."

"Thanks, Joshua. I'll tell him, but you know how he is. He probably won't take it from you unless you do it anonymously."

"Yeah, I do. Well, just let me know. You take care now." I leaned down, gave Rafe a big hug, and then limped down the alley feeling a bit lighter in my step, knowing I had helped my friends on the street get those thugs out of the way, even if only temporarily.

I found an old lawn chair someone had thrown out into the alley. Although it was bent, it would serve my purpose. Continuing on to the next street, I found a place on the sidewalk in the sun and plopped myself down to catch as many sun rays as possible.

With the sun's morning glow covering my face and beard, being as relaxed as I had been in weeks, my thoughts turned to my family, or at least what was left of my family. My 78-year-old mom was getting by with Social Security and a small pension from my dad. She was in reasonably good health, especially mentally. She was getting by, but my parents had lived in a tiny house. She was a little too much for me to handle in my current mental state, and I was a lot too much for her to handle with my anger issues. Thus, the street was the only place I felt comfortable.

My wife, or rather ex-wife, Janine, divorced me several months ago. She couldn't handle my temper and outbursts. She still loved me, but we could no longer be together. She had told me that she needed someone stable in her life. Our marriage had not produced any children since I had been deployed overseas so much, so that made the divorce a little easier.

Now, Janine's parents were a very different story. They always loved me, even after the divorce, and offered to help me several times. I didn't want to start depending on them or anyone else. I knew it wouldn't last. Sometimes, I still ran into them because they would drive around the area looking for me to see if they could help with anything. They had entered the stock market early and bought shares in Apple, Google, Amazon, and other companies when those stocks first started, making a pretty good fortune. I knew they always believed that Janine and I would or should get back together, but I didn't see that happening.

Mentally and physically, the injuries and problems from three tours in Afghanistan were never going to disappear. Doctors had tried to repair my leg and succeeded for the most part, but I still experienced pain and a limp. One enemy round had pierced my chest and one lung. I was mostly healed, but I no longer fully used that lung. Maybe some of the pain was just mental. Though I hadn't received a head wound, headaches came and went, and there wasn't much I could do to lessen their impact. I just had to endure them.

But now, sitting in the sun, with a relatively full stomach and the minimum amount of mental and physical pain, I was content, at least for the moment.

CHAPTER 4

The following morning

Marcie returned to the restaurant kitchen, where her sister Fran had just finished washing the breakfast dishes, and she wrapped her arms around her. "Thanks so much for the help this morning. Although it doesn't seem as busy as usual, there are a few regulars I didn't see at breakfast. I wonder if word got around about the altercation last night."

"That kind of thing can turn customers away," Fran replied. "Most of them have enough drama in their lives and don't need more when just trying to get a cheap meal. Don't you think you could increase your prices a little? Mom said you're barely breaking even."

"Most of my customers can barely afford what I charge now. If I raise the prices, I'll lose customers, and I don't want to do that to them."

"Maybe after things cool down, Marcie, customers will feel more comfortable returning. Time will tell."

The lunch crowd was light as usual, so for the rest of the afternoon, Marcie and her sister conducted an inventory to prepare for a shopping trip to restock the restaurant. Just before she expected the dinner crowd, Marcie heard the front doorbell jingle and entered the restaurant's dining area. It was her brother, John. "Welcome, little brother. What are you doing here today?"

"I haven't been by in a while, and I thought I'd try to get a free meal from you."

"You've probably heard about the trouble the other night and came to offer your support. I know you. But thanks anyway. And yes, I can give you a free meal for your kind and caring thoughts."

Walking over to John, she leaned over and hugged him. "How are you doing with this new chair? Is it easier to maneuver?"

"A little bit, but the whole chair is still stiff. It will take some time to get used to it."

"That's great. How long before you get your prosthetics?" Marcie knew this was a touchy subject for her brother, but she had told him several times that she was there to help him in any way she could.

Her brother, John, also a former Marine, was seriously injured in Afghanistan during an attack on his convoy. Although several members of his unit were killed in the attack, all his fellow soldiers in the Humvee he was driving, though seriously injured, survived. John was the most severely wounded, having lost both legs when the IED exploded under his side of the vehicle. One of his buddies not only saved his life but also the lives of the other crew members.

"So, what's for dinner?"

"Meatloaf tonight with mashed potatoes and green beans. Does that suit your fancy?"

"Absolutely. That's my favorite meal. You always make the best meatloaf."

"Thank you, my dear brother. I am your humble servant. You would probably eat it for every dinner if I made it that often," Marcie said as she entered the kitchen, returning a couple of minutes later with a full plate for her brother.

As John started eating dinner, Marcie sat with him, drinking coffee. Other customers entered, and her sister took care of their orders.

"So, sis, tell me about the other night. Someone told me you incapacitated four thugs from the street who were trying to rob you. I don't doubt your abilities, but that sounds a little far-fetched. What actually happened?"

"Thanks for your confidence in me, but I did have some help. Just before the incident, I encountered a homeless man in the alley, searching the dumpster for food. I invited him in and gave him a meal in the kitchen. When I heard glass break at the front of the restaurant, I rushed out and was confronted by three thugs. The homeless man came out of the kitchen and took all three on, taking them down in seconds."

"Wow. Who was this guy?"

"I don't know, but that's not the end of the story. A fourth man entered through the alley door and hit him over the head. I forgot to lock the door after letting the homeless man inside. This fourth guy was about to kick his face in when I slammed him in the back with a chair, knocking him down. The police arrived and took them away, but the homeless guy quickly slipped out the back door into the alley. He acted like he didn't want to be around the police."

"I was going to ask if you remember what your mom told you about letting strays into the restaurant, but I guess it was a good thing this time. Have you had any problems with the thugs since then?"

"No, but I heard from the police officer who responded that night that they had all bailed out of jail the next morning. The police are having a patrol come by during the evening, especially when I am getting ready to close, just in case they show up again."

"Yeah, I'm a little worried about that. How long are the cops going to be coming by?"

"Maybe for a while. The one cop asked me out to dinner, but I told him I was married. It didn't seem to put him off that much, however. I have brought my handgun in, so I have that now. I'll be careful."

"You know, we all worry about you having a restaurant in this location. I sure wish you could find a different place."

"If I weren't here, I wouldn't be able to help those families that need it, and finding a place to rent somewhere else would cost me even more. No. I will stay here and tough it out for a while longer."

"Okay, sis, but you just watch your back."

"I will. Now finish your dinner. I need to help Fran with the other customers."

As Marcie left her brother for him to finish eating, she attended to the few other customers in the restaurant. After he finished his meal, John waved at her and then rolled himself out the door that another customer had opened for him.

With the last customer having finished and left, Marcie started the restaurant clean-up before cleaning the kitchen. Fran had already left to go home to her family. Marcie had no family to get home to besides her mom, so she always stayed late to do the final cleaning and prep for the following day.

A shadow crossed the front windows as she prepared to go back to the kitchen. Turning quickly, she saw one of the thugs who had previously accosted her walking by, pointing a finger at her. This was not good. She rushed into the kitchen, grabbed her Glock 19, checked to make sure a round was in the chamber, and then went back into the restaurant. The thug was gone. She would need to keep her weapon close from now on and stay very alert to everything around her.

****

The following morning, just before Marcie headed out of her apartment to open her restaurant, her phone rang. She thought it was early for a phone call. Seeing the caller ID, she suspected it was her protective cop asking for another date. When she answered the phone, ready to turn him down again, she discovered that he was not calling for that reason.

"Marcie, this is Officer Duncan. I am at your restaurant. Your intrusion alarm notified us of a break-in. Then we received a call from a business across the street telling us it looked like your restaurant had been broken into. Are you all right?"

"Yes, I'm fine. The restaurant was okay when I left last night, but I saw one of those thugs walk by late in the evening. I'm on my way there now. Thanks for the call."

As Marcie hung up the phone, she sank into the nearest chair, crying. What was she going to do? She didn't have much extra money to fix much damage. Finally, lifting her head, she wiped away the tears. The Marines didn't teach her to give up at the slightest sign of trouble. She needed to get down there and assess what needed to be done.

Marcie realized the damage to the restaurant could have been worse. Some mirrors were broken, seat cushions were sliced, and pots and pans were thrown around the kitchen. Fortunately, the cold locker and other food storage rooms were always locked, and the thieves had not gained access, even though there were serious scratch marks and dents indicating an attempted break-in. She would need to close for a couple of days to get everything repaired, and she was worried this would reduce her customer base, as people might now be afraid to visit her restaurant. Shortly after calling her mom, she, her sister, and her brother, who had arrived, started cleaning up. Around mid-morning, some families who came for breakfast and found the restaurant closed returned to help her clean.

It took three days to get things back to the way they were. Officer Duncan contacted her, informing her that no evidence existed against the thugs she suspected of causing the damage. He also told her to invest in security cameras. She had told him she could not afford the cameras. She would have to pray that this was the end of the harassment.

****

I spent the next few nights under some makeshift shelters, but it was still cold. Fortunately, the rain had stopped. My meals were also a bit few and far between, so I decided to accept Marcie's offer of a hot meal whenever I needed one. I would soon find out if she were good at her word.

****

Marcie turned the closed sign outward, then locked the door. She had asked the window repairman if he could install additional locks on the front door that could only be opened with a key from inside or outside. This would prevent anyone from gaining access by breaking the window, reaching in, and unlocking a deadbolt. She also installed an extra lock on the alley's back door while he worked on it. She didn't want to be in the restaurant, cleaning up, and blindsided by someone breaking in through the back door.

Her Glock 19 was strapped around her waist, covered mainly by the bulky apron she had started wearing. She didn't want to upset her customers, but safety was now her highest priority. Marcie wished she could have afforded security cameras, but she didn't have much left after the window repair and the door security enhancements. She couldn't ask any of her family members for money, since they were about as financially strained as she was.

With the restaurant's eating area as clean as it would get that night, Marcie wrestled with how much later she wanted to stay to clean the kitchen. Her sister had stayed a couple of nights, but she had to leave early that evening. It was already 10 p.m. She had seen a patrol car drive by fifteen minutes earlier. It was probably Officer Duncan. She hadn't shown any signs in her behavior that she had seen his car. She hoped he wouldn't stop again to ask her out. Although she appreciated his help, he was not the kind of person she saw herself getting involved with.

It was time to take the trash to the alley and put it in the dumpster. Goosebumps ran up and down her arms every evening she thought about this task. First, she unlocked the two locks, then pulled out her Glock and slowly opened the door to check the alley before grabbing the garbage sack. She didn't want to have both hands full if she was attacked. The alley was empty except for a lone figure shuffling toward her from the far end.

Keeping her eye on the individual and checking behind her in case this was a distraction, Marcie moved fifteen feet toward the dumpster. This was going to be tricky. She had to use both hands to lift the heavy dumpster lid, which meant holstering her weapon. That would be the time she would be the most defenseless.

As Marcie tried to decide how to handle the situation, she quickly moved back to the kitchen door and waited for this person to pass. She backed up, left the trash bag by the dumpster, and pointed her Glock downward, gripping it with both hands. It was dark enough where she was that when the person approached, she assumed it was him based on his size; he wouldn't see her weapon until it was too late. When she first entered the alley, she also propped open the door to provide a quick escape if needed. She was always taught in the Marines to have multiple escape plans, but her surroundings limited her options in this case. A small shaft of light behind her backlit her, making her weapon invisible.

****

Noting the time on a clock in a store window, I passed by as I headed toward the alley behind the restaurant; I saw it was nearing 10 p.m. I needed to hurry if I wanted to catch Marcie still cleaning up. When I entered the alley, I was nearly a block from the dumpster near the door into her restaurant. As I shuffled as fast as I could, I saw a shaft of light lance into the alley. I figured she was probably taking out the trash, just like she had the first time I saw her. I needed to hurry.

As I approached her, I noticed that she had dropped the garbage bag next to the dumpster and had backed up to the slightly ajar door. Her arms were hanging straight down, with her hands in front of her.

I instinctively knew what she was holding; it was a weapon of some kind, even though I could not see it.

Now only twenty feet from her, I called out, "Good evening, Marcie. Am I too late for one of your great leftover meals?" I could see Marcie's posture relax as she raised one hand holding the weapon and returned it to the holster on her hip.

"You scared me for a moment, Joshua. You haven't been around for a while, but to answer your question, of course, I have a meal for you. First, though, you need to work for it."

I stood there momentarily speechless until she continued, "Would you open this dumpster and throw that sack of garbage in? It would be a big help for me."

Coming out of my frozen position, I responded, "Of course." Then, moving forward, I quickly lifted the dumpster lid and threw the bulky, heavy bag of garbage into it.

"All right then. Come in, and I'll see what I can find. How have you been?" She asked as she led me into her kitchen.

"Not too bad. With the rain gone, it's a bit easier." Reaching to remove a scarf from a hook where her aprons were hanging, Marcie handed it to me, saying, "I think you forgot this last time you were here in your rush to leave."

"Thanks so much. I didn't remember where I had left it. It is an essential piece of clothing in this kind of weather."

Laying the scarf on the table, I watched Marcie bustle around the kitchen, pulling some chicken out of the fridge and opening some containers. She stacked mashed potatoes and corn on a plate. During the two minutes the plate was in the microwave, she brought me a large mug full of coffee. "No cream or sugar, right?" she asked.

"Right. Thank you." I leaned back in my chair, taking a moment to relax at the rare opportunity this young lady provided. Although I recalled the last time I was here, it hadn't ended up so relaxing.

"So, have you heard from those gang bangers since I was here last?" As Marcie turned toward me, I could tell by the look on her face that she had. "What happened?"

"They came back a few nights ago and trashed the place. It took nearly all my savings to fix it, including adding extra security to the doors. They got out of jail the morning after they were arrested, and the night before the break-in. I saw one of them walk by after I closed, staring at me as he passed. He pointed his finger at me like it was a gun."

I could feel the anger rising in me as I clenched my fists. Keeping my voice calm, I said, "That's not right. Are the police doing anything?"

"Oh, they drive by occasionally, but I don't know if that will do much good." Marcie opened the microwave after it dinged, removed the plate, and set it down in front of Joshua. She then pulled up a chair to the same table.

As I sat still, not touching my food, I could feel the anger on my face and wondered what Marcie must think of me in this state. Before I could pick up my fork to take my first bite, the headache struck me. It felt like someone had put my head in a vise, squeezing tighter and tighter. I clasped my hands around my head, bending over in the chair with debilitating pain. As I felt myself falling to the floor, Marcie's arms partially caught me, lowering me more gently than I would have gone alone. Lying on the floor, shaking with pain, I put my hands on my head to try to hide the tears of pain from Marcie, while I could still feel her hands stroking my head.

I didn't know how long I had been lying on the floor because, like in past incidents where I often lost consciousness from the pain, I suspected I had fainted again this time. When I opened my eyes, a blanket was over me, and Marcie sat on the floor next to me.

"Are you all right, Joshua? You scared me. I was going to call for an ambulance, but because of how you reacted last time when the police came, I suspected you wouldn't want me to. What happened?"

"Headaches. Excruciating headaches. I have had them periodically since I returned from the desert. They don't last very long, and doctors have all said it was part of the PTSD that I suffer." Throwing the blanket back, with Marcie's help, I pushed myself up off the floor and sat back into the chair. Marcie grabbed my plate and stuck it back in the microwave for another minute.

Finally, recovering from the headache attack, it didn't take me long to finish the plate of food, at which time I sat back with a satisfied sigh. "You have been kinder than words can describe, Marcie. I wish there was something I could do for you. Is there anything, anything at all that I can do to pay you back?"

Marcie's response told me I had hit a touchy point with her. "No," she stated with some mild anger in her voice. "I don't do things like this for payback. I get great satisfaction from just helping people like you. That is why I have this restaurant in this location. Do you see that? Do you understand that?"

"I am so sorry to have upset you. I have never experienced the kindness and compassion you've shown me or most of my veteran friends on the street. Thank you."

Marcie's face softened as she declared, "I didn't mean to get on your case, Joshua. I like to help. I'm a bit driven to help others. That is all the payment I need, knowing I have helped people for one more day in their lives."

"And know that everyone greatly appreciates that, Marcie, including me, even though we might not say so."

I could tell Marcie understood as she turned to continue the final kitchen cleanup, which included my plate and coffee mug. As she took off her apron, she suddenly stopped and turned toward me with her hands on her hips.

"All right. You want to do something for me. I have an offer to make to you," she grinned.

I sat up straighter in my chair, a bit surprised by her comment and change of attitude. "Shoot," I said.

"You want to pay me back for the meals. Okay. You come back here every evening at closing time. I'll feed you dinner. Then you spend the night on a cot I will set up for you. You will be my security guard. But there is one problem." She paused as she thought about how to say what she was thinking. Finally, she just said it. "You actually do stink." She had an even bigger grin on her face. "So, there is a bathroom with a shower through that door over there," she said as she pointed to a door next to the small walk-in freezer. "You must shower and use the washer and dryer to clean your clothes. In the morning, you leave before customers arrive, and you can take something with you for breakfast. How does that sound?"

CHAPTER 5

I sat still, stunned. I was shaken to my core by Marcie's offer.

"I don't think I am capable of that," I said. "I haven't been very responsible with my life lately, and I'm not sure I can handle that responsibility."

Marcie remained standing, hands on her hips. "You need a good meal once a day at least. It would be best to have a safe place to sleep at night. I am offering you both of those. You asked me if there was anything, *and I emphasize anything* you could do for me. Well, that's the best I can think of, requiring the least effort from you. If you think it is too much for you to handle, fine. I will risk those thugs returning and destroying my restaurant next time." She knew this would get to my ego.

Rubbing my hands over my face and through my long black hair, I finally sat up straight in the chair. "Okay. You have a deal. I hope you're not putting too much faith in me. I haven't been responsible for much of anything for quite some time."

"It's better than what I have now, and I can't afford security cameras. If those guys show up again, you can leave after the police are called because I know you want no contact with the police, although I don't know why," she continued, standing with a questioning look on her face.

"I've done some things I'm not proud of, and the cops might be looking for me for some of those actions. I can't take the risk that they are. I can't end up in jail. That would be the end of me."

"Okay, Josh. I understand. So, do you want to start tonight? I'm about finished cleaning up, and there is a cot in the back room. There may even be a blanket and pillow for it. I'll check. But it would be best if you cleaned up and washed your clothes after I left. Can you do that?"

"Guess I am going to have to, ma'am," I uttered as I stood, stretched myself, and headed to a back storage closet to look for the cot. I found it folded up in a corner, so I brought it out and found a place near the bathroom to open it. Then, opening the bathroom door, I looked in to inspect it. It was larger than I thought, with a generously sized shower, and the room was spotlessly clean.

"I'm leaving now," Marcie shouted at me as she headed toward the front door. "Turn out the lights and make sure both doors are secured. There is a phone on the wall in the restaurant area and one in the kitchen, so use whichever is most convenient. If something happens, dial 911, provide the information and address, and then you can leave before the police arrive. The intrusion alarm will also alert the police, so you can leave whether or not you call the police. If you have time, please contact me; otherwise, the police will reach out. Please don't go too far; I will let you back in after everyone is gone. Hopefully, nothing will happen, but you don't need to put yourself in harm's way like you did the other night."

I watched Marcie leave, then locked the door behind her. I turned off all the front lights, leaving only one small light in the kitchen and the bathroom. I couldn't remember the last time I had a real shower in a proper bathroom. It felt strange. And what was I supposed to do with my beard and hair? I could tie my hair back, but should I keep my beard? My veteran friends out on the street wouldn't recognize me without the beard when I returned, and I was sure that would happen. This was only a temporary diversion. I didn't expect it to last long.

****

Marcie entered her tiny house, which her parents had owned before her dad's death and was now shared jointly by Marcie and her mom. Her mom couldn't handle it financially on her own. Marcie could still smell the dinner her mom had prepared earlier in the evening. The aroma of garlic and tomato sauce filled the air. She knew her mom had made enough for several people, as she had learned from working at the restaurant that making small portions was not her mom's style.

"About time you got here," Maxine chided. "I was starting to get a little worried."

"I got delayed a little," Marcie replied. She wasn't sure how her mom would take to the idea that she had taken on Joshua to watch the place at night. She would eventually find out, so she may as well tell her up front.

"Mom, please don't get upset, but do you remember that veteran I told you about who helped me with those gang guys a while back? Well, he came back tonight, and I fixed him dinner again. He wanted to pay me back for the meals, so I took him on as a security guard at night in return for dinner each night and something to eat before he left in the morning."

"You did what!" her mom hollered at her. "Do you know what kind of trouble you could bring crashing down on your head? You don't even know this guy."

"Mom, I think I'm a pretty good judge of character, and he seems all right. I can't afford to do anything else, and I feel very safe with him. I told him he had to shower, wash his clothes, and be gone by morning before customers arrived. I think it will be okay."

"Oh, my goodness. You have always been your own person, so I guess I'll have to go along with your judgment. Please, just be careful around him. You should ask him more about his background and obtain his full name, so that if something goes wrong, the police can locate him. Will you do that for me?"

"Yes, Mother, I will do that," Marcie stated, frustration in her voice. "Now, I am tired, so I am heading to bed. I will see you in the morning."

Then, hugging her mom and kissing her cheek, she headed upstairs to her room. It was the same room she had slept in before going off to the Marines. Her walls were still plastered with Marine recruiting posters, and various awards from her service time were hung in frames along with pictures of members of her unit—those who were living and those who had given their lives for their country.

Every time she stood looking at those photos, tears welled in her eyes for her comrades who had to be carried off the plane in metal boxes. There were far too many of them. She knew some of the survivors probably had significant adjustment problems. She felt fortunate to have her mother, brother, and sister for support when she returned. That made all the difference in the world.

She didn't even feel like taking a shower tonight. She could do that in the morning. Desperately needing sleep, she threw her clothes in a pile, pulled on shorts and a T-shirt, climbed under the covers, and was out almost before she could say her prayers. The following day, thinking back to the past evening, she couldn't even remember how many of her nightly prayers she had completed.

****

After stepping out of the shower onto the towel I had placed on the floor as a mat, I dried off, realizing I looked like a lobster because I had run the water so hot and stayed under that steaming downpour for so long. Some of the dirt had been harder to clean off myself than it would be to clean an old cast-iron skillet left out in the rain. I was sure some skin came off with the dirt.

While drying my hair, I noticed an elastic hair tie left in the bathroom. It could have been Marcie's, since her hair was long enough for it, or maybe her sister's, or a customer's, although I doubted she would let customers use this bathroom. Tying my hair back in a ponytail, I looked at myself in the mirror. My beard was a real mess. It was clean now, but still looked pretty rough. I didn't want to cut it all off, but maybe I could trim it to look tidier and less like a buffalo or a bear.

Out in the kitchen, I noticed a pair of scissors hanging on a hook. After grabbing them, I started trimming my beard. It took me about 30 minutes, but after my makeshift job, I found it much easier to manage, and I began to see my true self. It was a strange sight. With the towel still wrapped around my waist, I grabbed my clothes and headed to the washer. Everything I needed was there, although I was worried I'd have to run my clothes through the cycle a couple of times to get them really clean.

Surprisingly, the first cycle did a respectable job, so I threw them into the dryer and went into the kitchen to look for something to eat. That wasn't part of the agreement, but what would a little snack hurt? I was already hungry, and with my lifestyle, even though I had an arrangement here at this restaurant, things could change in an instant, leaving me back out on the street.

As I reached for the refrigerator door, I heard the front door rattling, as if someone was checking whether it was locked. Peering cautiously around the corner into the restaurant, I didn't see a police car outside, and the figure I could make out in the dark looked suspicious. I turned around and flipped on the kitchen light to scare the person away. When I looked again, it seemed to work. The figure had moved out of sight. I needed to get dressed. If I tried to defend this place, or myself, in my birthday suit, it wouldn't end well for me.

Finally, the dryer buzzed, signaling that my clothes were dry— or at least mostly dry. I wouldn't wait for them to be completely dry before getting dressed. I had spent many nights in wet clothes, and at least these were warm right out of the dryer. They felt good. With the lights off, I cautiously moved into the restaurant, walking around the side to approach the front. After Marcie left for the night, I had double-locked the front door, and everything still felt secure. I couldn't see anyone on the street, but I knew it would be different if I checked the back alley, because several friends shared food from this restaurant's dumpster.

As tempting as it was to see if anyone was out in the alley looking for a meal and then give them something from the fridge, I knew that would violate Marcie's trust in me. I could not do that to her. Judging a person's character was not about how a person acted when others were watching, but how he or she acted when no one was watching. Those sayings and the Bible were what supported me and guided my behavior. They always had and always would. Although I had done things that went against the teachings of the Good Book at times, it was only when necessary for my survival, and I always felt guilty afterward.

The clock on the kitchen wall reflected 12:30 a.m. It was time to hit the sack since I had to be up and out early in the morning. Tomorrow, whenever I encountered any of my friends back out on the street, I needed to come up with a plausible story to explain my improved appearance. I wouldn't let anyone abuse Marcie's hospitality for as long as it lasted, so I wasn't about to share my experiences with her with my friends.

CHAPTER 6

While grabbing a few pieces of fruit from a bowl in the fridge the following morning, I saw Marcie's car slide into a parking place across the street. I had already stowed the cot, blanket, and pillow back into the closet, but I wanted to leave the restaurant before she entered. Until now, she had not asked me many questions about my past, and I wasn't prepared to discuss it. When I heard the front door unlock, I exited out the back, locking and closing the alley door behind me. I wondered if Marcie would give me a key at some point. Not anytime soon, I was sure. She may be trusting, given that both of us are Marines, but not that trusting. With an apple stuffed in my pocket for later and a half-eaten banana, I headed down the alley in a rare, good mood.

After turning the corner from the alley onto a quiet secondary street, I saw my friend Rafe sitting against a building, dozing in the warm sun. Deciding I could spare the apple, I walked up to him and grabbed him by the back of the neck. Rafe jerked awake, ready to defend himself against an attack, until he looked up into my smiling eyes.

"Man, don't do that to me! You scared me enough to almost force me up out of this chair and run down the street, peeing my pants on the way." Pausing with a sadder look on his face, he added, "Oh, if I could only do that."

By this point, we were both laughing hysterically. I pulled the apple from my pocket and handed it to Rafe. "Here's a little morning snack for you, my friend. Fresh off the tree."

"Yeah, right," Rafe responded. "As cold as this apple is, if it was fresh off a tree, that tree would have to have been growing in Alaska or the Arctic."

"Okay, you got me. I got it from the restaurant down the alley."

"Are you going back there again? What's up with that?"

"I don't want to say too much, but I'm helping the owner keep an eye on her place in return for an occasional meal. Don't spread that around, though."

Looking up and down and sniffing at my clothes, he said, "That explains your upgraded appearance and clean clothes. Sounds like a good gig."

"Probably won't last long, but it is to keep those thugs from tearing the place up as they did once already. The lady needs help, so why not for a little while?"

"I don't suppose this lady owner is a doll, is she? Well, of course she is. That's why you have this sh*t-eating grin."

"Yes, she is a real cutie and an ex-Marine, and she needed help. You know as well as I do that it won't go anywhere. It is just nice to be treated kindly for a change."

"I hear you, my friend. Oh, before I forget, you need to lie low a bit. Some guy was hanging around last night with a photo of you, asking questions. The photo didn't do you justice. You were clean-shaven in uniform. I don't know if he was a cop or a private dick, but he was nicely dressed."

"Thanks, Rafe. I don't know why anyone would be out looking for me except for the cops. The stuff I've done has been very minor, and most of it was months ago. Ask some questions if you see him or anyone else looking for me. Find out what's going on. Okay?"

"Will do. Thanks for the apple. Take care of yourself," Rafe said as I headed back into the alley from which I had just come.

Wonder what that was all about, I thought to myself. I had stolen a few small things over the months and broken into several abandoned buildings, but nothing serious enough to draw anyone's attention. I knew of an abandoned auto repair shop that had shut down a couple of months earlier, where I could probably hide out until evening. It was only a couple of blocks away, and I tried to spend a night there once, but all the doors were locked. Maybe this time, I could find another way in.

On high alert to my surroundings, I passed Marcie's restaurant across the street and down the alley that continued for another block. At the corner, I turned, keeping to the sidewalk closest to the buildings for a block, then turned again down another alley that I knew would bring me to the rear of the repair shop. Although all the doors were bolted and locked, I finally found a place where I could pull out part of the metal siding on the alley side of the building to give me access to the building's empty vehicle bay.

This part of the building was semi-dark, where vehicles were once hoisted up for repair. I saw no signs of anyone else taking up housekeeping here, so I was alone, which was how I liked it. I needed to find a place to nap and rest until evening. By getting some extra sleep during the day, I could stay up later at the restaurant to watch for anyone trying to break in, which might have happened last night if I hadn't been there.

Inside the auto repair shop, I found furniture still in place, along with all kinds of paper products, a computer, and a printer. It was as if the owner had abandoned the place, leaving no one to claim it. What caught my attention next was a giant, overstuffed recliner that could also serve as a bed. I had lucked out. Hopefully, no one else would discover this spot. The entrance I used wasn't secure, so I needed to check if I could find something to block the opening after I got inside to hide it. That might keep other intruders out.

Climbing back out of the hole in the building, I discovered some discarded boxes sitting next to a dumpster, so I carried them over and set them in front of the hole. Then, crawling through the hole, I pulled the boxes in place to cover the entry. Back inside the auto body shop, I found a piece of wire in a tool cabinet, which I wound around the end of a screw that used to hold that piece of siding closed. I pulled it tight and secured it around a nail sticking out of a two-by-four. The boxes outside were not up against the building, but they would conceal this slightly misshapen metal siding from any casual inspection. I prayed it would work.

It was finally time for a nap. The lounge/desk chair looked as comfortable as it seemed, and within moments, I was in dreamland. My last thought before drifting off was a prayer that this retreat would last for a while.

For the next several nights, I served as a night watchman at the restaurant and was rewarded with some outstanding dinners. Marcie did notice my improved appearance and grooming efforts. One night, during her cleanup and prep for the following day, the inevitable query about my life, my parents, and my service time began. At first, I was hesitant to discuss myself, and she never pushed the issue, but that night, I broke down and voluntarily talked to her about myself.

I had just finished a huge plate of lasagna and was placing my dishes in the kitchen sink when Marcie came back from cleaning up in the restaurant. "So, you have asked me about my background," I said, glancing at her, "but until now, I've kept a relatively closed mouth. You've been so kind and generous to me that I owe you."

I told Marcie about the small twelve-acre farm I had grown up on, with cows, horses, pigs, chickens, geese, fruit trees, and a truck garden. Once I got talking, I could hardly hold back. My childhood was very calm, and I lived in a loving family. I was involved in a couple of fights in high school over a girl—actually, over two girls—but by then I had grown to my full height and was close to two hundred pounds, and not many of the guys in my class were willing to challenge me physically. Also, with that height and weight, it wasn't easy to convince the football coach that I wasn't interested in playing.

After high school, I completed two years of college but did not fit in. The day a U.S. Marine Recruiter came to the campus, he enamored me. One question led to another, which led to some testing and, ultimately, a signed contract. Then, it was off to Parris Island for basic training. My mother was unhappy when I entered the Marines, but my father had been in the Air Force. Although he had tried talking me into joining the Air Force instead, he accepted that his son wanted to serve his country in the Marines, especially after 9/11.

Marcie sat, seemingly transfixed by my story. When she asked about my overseas deployments, I shut down and told her there was nothing significant, just that I was wounded and sent home with PTSD, a bum leg, headaches, and a discharge.

"It's getting late," I pointed out to Marcie. "Your family is going to be getting worried about you if you don't get a move on."

"Oh, my goodness. You're right. Can we talk some more tomorrow night? I want to hear your story."

"Not much more to it," I commented, "But you can tell me about yourself next time." This was my way of avoiding any more talk about myself, which I was not comfortable with, especially about what happened in Afghanistan. Dragging up those memories inevitably brought my PTSD roaring to the surface.

"Okay, I'm done. I will see you tomorrow night. Thanks for all your help." Marcie adjusted her Glock on her hip, put on her coat, and headed out the front door. I followed her to lock up behind her. She looked up and down the street before she crossed to her car, turning back to look, smile, and wave at me as she entered her car.

The following day, after another quiet night, I prepared to leave through the back door before Marcie showed up. During the night, no strangers rattled the door or tried to break in. My job had been easy so far and hardly worth the meals she provided, but I would keep doing it if it gave her some peace of mind. She had told me the trial or hearing for the four thugs who attacked her was only two weeks away, so she'd be glad to get it over with. She asked if I would consider testifying for her, but I declined, saying it would be too high-profile for me. I hoped they'd get jail or prison time without my testimony, but that might be too much to expect given how the local courts work.

Several more days passed with no incidents. I had also not

heard of anyone else searching for me with my photograph. That was the best news yet. I continued to hole up in the abandoned auto repair shop during the day, and no one else had found a way in, so I had the place all to myself.

That evening, after getting several hours of sleep in my

new lounge chair, I wormed my way out through the small

opening and pushing the cardboard boxes back in place. I stood and made my way to the end of the alley. My leg hadn't bothered me as much lately, but it still hurt. Starting across the street, I glanced at my watch to ensure I would not arrive too early at Marcie's. I heard a shout and looked up to see Wolf flying at me, knocking me back onto the sidewalk, which wasn't easy due to my size.

I was stunned, but saw a dark SUV speeding past us down the street. Wolf was lying partly on the sidewalk and partly in the street. He was not moving. I crawled over to him on my hands and knees, slowly rolling him over onto his back to better assess him. He was unconscious; there was blood on his forehead where he had hit the concrete, and one leg looked deformed, possibly broken.

I put my arms beneath Wolf's arms and stood, pulling him out of the street and onto the sidewalk. I checked his breathing and found it all right. *What to do now,* I thought. I couldn't leave Wolf on the sidewalk, and I had no phone to call for help. Just then, I heard a door open a few doors down from me, where a shop owner was closing for the night.

"Help! Help!" I hollered. "Can you call 911? This man has been hit by a car!"

The man looked around as if he was looking for someone else who could make the call so he wouldn't have to, but finding no one, he responded, "Sure. I can do that."

I sat with Wolf for ten minutes until an ambulance rolled up. Wolf had regained consciousness, but the pain he was in was evident on his face. Unfortunately, I couldn't do anything about that. Once the medics arrived, I escaped back down the alley before the police arrived. I was late getting to Marcie's and hoped she was still there.

I had to walk several blocks out of my way to avoid the scene with Wolf, but I finally made it to the alley at the back of the restaurant. Trying the door, I found it locked, so I rapped on it several times. I waited a full minute, thinking maybe Marcie was either in the restaurant section cleaning up or had already gone home. Finally deciding to risk showing myself on the front street, I walked to the front entrance.

As I leaned against the front window to peer in, I noticed a light on in the back of the restaurant where the kitchen was located, but I didn't see Marcie moving around. That's when I realized the front door was splintered and slightly ajar. Pushing the door open, I hurried into the restaurant and was hit with a scene that made my stomach turn. Marcie was lying on the floor in a messy heap, with torn clothes and blood covering most of her face and clothes. I had failed. I had let her down when she depended on me.

Rushing to her and kneeling, I pressed my fingers against her carotid artery to check if she was alive, not expecting to feel a pulse. There was one, but it was faint. She had lost a considerable amount of blood, and every second counted if she was going to survive this attack. I sprinted into the kitchen and tore open the front cover of the large first-aid kit I had noticed bolted to the wall. Grabbing gauze and anything else that might help stop the bleeding, I hurried back to Marcie, who remained unconscious on the floor.

Applying direct pressure to her head wound, I finally stopped the bleeding and wrapped the gauze multiple times around her head to secure the pressure bandage. I couldn't find any other significant sources of bleeding.

Now standing, I rushed over to the wall phone, picked up the receiver, and dialed 911. After giving the necessary information, I let the phone hang and went back to Marcie, who was now moaning on the floor. She could go into shock if I left her like this, so I grabbed the blanket and pillow I used at night and returned to her, making her as comfortable as possible. As the ambulance and police arrived, I leaned down, softly kissed Marcie's bloody forehead and whispered, "You're going to be okay. I will take care of this. They won't ever do this to anyone again. I will be back."

Standing, I limped to the back door, unlocked it, and pulled it shut behind me as I shuffled down the alley. When I was done with them, they'd wish they'd never gotten out of jail and would wish they were in hell compared to what I was about to put them through.

CHAPTER 7

After I had moved across the street, traveling a roundabout route so I could view the front of Marcie's restaurant, I observed another civilian vehicle arrive, its tires squealing on the pavement as it slammed to a stop. One person who got out of the car looked like Marcie's sister. I had seen her once hugging Marcie as she left the restaurant on her way home after helping clean up. The other individual was probably her brother, since he was in a wheelchair, although I had never seen him before. From this vantage point, I couldn't get much of a look at him due to the lack of light and my distance from the restaurant. Since it was a crime scene, the police did not permit them inside the restaurant, but a few minutes after they arrived, the EMTs wheeled a gurney out with Marcie strapped to it. I could see that her head wasn't covered, indicating she was still alive. Marcie's sister and brother escorted her to the ambulance, then backed off as the EMTs loaded her inside.

I had seen enough. I would hang around until everyone left, then try to get back in to spend the night. After that, I didn't know how I would track down the individuals who had done this to Marcie, but I was determined to find a way. I didn't fully grasp why I felt compelled to avenge Marcie. Maybe it was because we were both Marines. Perhaps it was to repay her for all her kindness toward me. It didn't matter. Whatever the reason, I would dedicate my time to finding them, no matter what it took.

It was an hour after the ambulance left before the police finally finished their investigation, and everyone departed. After making sure everyone was gone from the area and I wouldn't be seen, I crossed the street to the front door. It looked securely locked, so I walked to the corner, then into the alley, and approached the door near the dumpster. Not surprisingly, given the first responders' activity, no one had thought to lock this door, and I was able to get in. I was tired, and it had been a long night. My main goal before heading out on my new mission in the morning was to eat and then sleep. I no longer had a blanket or pillow, as I had used them to make Marcie more comfortable, but I found a couple of tablecloths to use as substitutes. No sooner had I laid down on the cot that I pulled out of the closet than I fell into a restless sleep.

Despite all that had occurred that night, I still managed several hours of sleep. As it turned out, I slept a little too long because I awoke to voices in the restaurant. Jerking up on the cot, I grabbed my boots and slipped them on without tying them. As I contemplated how I would get out of the alley door without being seen, I found I was too late.

"Who are you? What are you doing here?" Marcie's sister shouted as she defensively held a broom in her hands.

"I'm sorry," I uttered. "I'm Joshua. Marcie lets me sleep here at night to watch the place." I sat back down on the cot to avoid appearing threatening.

"Well, where were you last night?"

By this time, Marcie's mother had walked up behind Fran and asked the same question. "If you were supposed to provide security, why weren't you here?" Both women stood with their hands on their hips in demanding poses.

"I am so very sorry, ladies. A veteran friend of mine was hit by a car last night. He managed to push me out of the way, but he didn't escape injury. I took care of him until the police came, then I immediately headed over here. That's when I found Marcie."

"So, you are Joshua," Maxine said as her features softened. "Marcie told us about you. Are you the one who bandaged her head and covered her?"

"Yes, I did. There wasn't much else I could do other than call 911. How is she?"

"She survived the night but is in a coma. She had a severe head wound and concussion. The next forty-eight hours will reveal more," Fran said. "You shouldn't be here. There's no longer any need for security. We don't know when Marcie will be able to return, if at all. Please leave."

"Can I ask if the police have found anything that points to who was responsible for this attack? Was it the same people who broke in that first night when I confronted them?"

"They didn't give us much information. I thought they suspected it was the same people."

"Thank you. I will get out of your hair. Tell Marcie when she wakes up that I will be praying for her swift recovery and the punishment for her attackers." As I reached down to tie my boots under the watchful eyes of Maxine and Fran, my mind raced around with various thoughts. Since the back door had been unlocked last night, Marcie's attackers likely exited that way so no one on the street would see them. Some friends often hang around this area, and perhaps one of them could provide some information. I had to start somewhere. It might as well be there.

Standing up, I folded the cot and the two tablecloths I had used as a blanket, then put them away in the storage closet. After slipping on my worn Stetson, I touched my hand to the brim and nodded at the two ladies in a sign of respect, then turned and exited through the back door. First, I needed to check on Wolf after last night's accident. Then, I would begin my search.

Since I had left the restaurant in such a rush, I hadn't managed to get anything to eat, so the hunger pangs were setting in. This wasn't a new feeling; I had been there many times before. On my way to the hospital to check on Wolf, I found an unlocked bathroom at a nearby gas station. Not wanting to draw attention when I entered the hospital, I washed my face and brushed my hair and beard to look presentable.

Just after entering the hospital, I saw a pay phone on the wall, so I walked over, pulled a quarter out of my pocket, and dialed the hospital information number. If I had gone to the desk, a nurse or administrator probably would have asked for my ID. Since I planned to pose as Rafe's brother, I figured I might get away with the ruse on the phone.

"Yes, I am inquiring about my brother, Wolf. He was involved in a hit-and-run last night, and I want to visit him. Can you tell me what room he is in?" I did not know Wolf's real or last name. We usually didn't share that kind of detail on the street.

Amazingly, the nurse did not ask me any further questions and provided me with the room number on the third floor. It was not in the intensive care unit, but was close to it. That information told me that Wolf was not too seriously injured.

After waiting for an empty elevator, I entered, reached the third floor, and exited, looking for signs pointing me to the right hallway. When I turned and walked down the corridor, I passed the ICU. I wondered if that was where Marcie was being cared for. After seeing Wolf, I might find out if I could get in to see her.

Peering into the open door to room 315, I saw Wolf sitting up in bed, and the room was otherwise empty. As I entered, I said, "If you keep misbehaving like this, my friend, they will have to name a wing of this hospital after you."

"Hey, my careless friend. You're the one who should be in here."

"I know. I know. You saved my life. It was about time. I've pulled your sorry ass out of the fire a couple of times out there."

As I walked up to the bed, I reached down, shook Wolf's hand, and then pulled him into a bear hug with both of us laughing.

"How are you doing, brother? You don't look too bad."

"Nah. I'll be out of here tomorrow. I'll be on crutches, actually, just one crutch, since I can't use my left arm after shoulder surgery. I wrenched my knee but didn't break anything. Are you okay? Sorry if I hit you too hard."

"No, man. I'm fine. Not a scratch."

"Did they find that rig that ran us down?"

"Not that I know of. I think I know who it was. Some gang members have targeted the restaurant I've been helping out at, and they just put the owner in the hospital. They should be in jail, but now she can't testify against them. They might have been after me, too, since I was helping her."

"You had better watch yourself, friend. Stay low and out of sight for a while."

"Not going to happen, Wolf. That restaurant owner was a Marine. I will find those who did this to her. By the way, you know some ex-cops, don't you?"

"Yeah. Why?"

"I need to get the identities of the guys they arrested the first time they broke into the restaurant, but I can't openly get involved. You told me someone has been circulating a photo of me, so I need to stay in the shadows, but I am going after them. When you leave, will you check for me and see if you can provide some info?"

"I'll do what I can. Where do you want to meet when and if I come up with something?"

"Come to that restaurant with a back door in the alley by dumpster number seventeen. Come after 10 p.m. If they let me, I will try to help them clean up the mess and spend the next few nights there."

"Okay. Will do."

I figured I had overstayed my visit to the hospital and wanted to leave before a nurse or doctor appeared. "See you later, my friend." I shook Wolf's hand again, then left the room. As I continued down the hall and paused at the ICU door, I looked through the glass panel. Only one nurse was on duty, and she was facing away from me. This might be my only chance to check on Marcie.

Slowly pushing the swinging door open, I slipped in as quietly as possible, then turned right down the first hall. Now out of the nurse's sight, I peeked into each room. When I reached the fourth room, I saw Marcie lying in the bed, and then I noticed her name printed on the white plastic board at the edge of the door.

Aside from Marcie, the room was empty, but I didn't want to get caught in there and have to answer many questions. Approaching her bedside, I saw the vital sign monitors all beeping in unison, but Marcie appeared to be sleeping, or maybe still in a coma. As I leaned down, I whispered into her ear. "I'm sorry, Marcie. I will find them." I then kissed her on the forehead, and as I turned to leave, I heard her moan slightly. Maybe this was the reverse of the prince kissing the frog. It was the frog kissing the prince. Turning my head as I exited the room, I saw that Marcie was still prone in the bed, with the Vital Signs Monitor the only sound.

When I pushed through the ICU doors, I heard a voice behind me shout, "Hey, there! Wait!" But I was already out the door and headed down the hall toward the bank of elevators. Now, though, I didn't want to wait for an elevator and have someone catch up to me, so instead I found the stairs and took them down as fast as my bum leg would carry me. The closest door was not the one through which I had entered the hospital, but it would do. I headed across the parking lot into a nearby business park containing numerous abandoned buildings, any of which I could hide in if necessary.

****

Back in the hospital, the middle-aged doctor wearing his white lab coat and a stethoscope around his neck stood in the open doorway of the ICU, watching the man run down the hallway. He pulled a photograph out of his pocket and mentally compared it with what he had seen of the unidentified man who had just rushed out of the ICU. He was sure it was the same person. A phone number was written on the back of the photo. He walked over to the nurses' station to make the call.

****

It took an hour to get back to my neighborhood, which I called home, by taking a roundabout route to make sure I wasn't followed. I had things to do, and jail was not part of my plan. My main goal was to find Rafe and have him spread the word about who I was searching for. My friends on the street, especially those who had served their country, and my fellow Marine brothers would be a big help in achieving my mission. I felt good about myself for the first time in a long while. I had a goal. An objective. A reason to keep going.

Arriving back at my alley behind the restaurant, I tried the door but found it locked. So, against my better judgment, I knocked. It took several knocks before I heard the lock turn. When it swung open, Maxine and her daughter, Fran, were standing there.

"What do you want?" Maxine asked, her face stern.

"I thought maybe you could use a little help cleaning up. Marcie was so generous and thoughtful with me that I owe you both at least that. Please let me help."

Maxine and Fran looked at each other, and then as they wiped sweat off their foreheads, I could see in their expressions that they realized they could use some help. Stepping aside, Maxine said, "Come on in. This is very kind of you. I guess if Marcie could trust you, so can we."

Walking past them, I took my hat, which I had previously removed when the women had opened the door, and pulled off my jacket, setting it on a chair. "Where do you want me to start?"

CHAPTER 8

Thanks to Maxine and Fran's help, the restaurant was back to its usual self by dinnertime. Fran had gone to a hardware store to purchase additional supplies to my specifications.

"Maxine, it looks like you'll be ready for customers tomorrow," I observed as I sat in a chair for the first time that day after I had started cleaning and repairing. "I would appreciate a quick bite to eat before I go."

"Of course. You have certainly earned it today. Fran, get that plate of fried chicken out of the fridge. It is a day or two old, but Marcie's chicken is always good."

"I love it cold," I asserted. It was way better than anything I would find out on the street. "If it's all right, I have some errands to run, so if you could put it in a sack, I will take it to go."

"Aren't you going to spend the night here?"

"I don't think so for at least a couple of nights. As I mentioned earlier, I have some errands to run at night. But thank you for the offer. I will knock on the back door when I return to spend the night and keep an eye on the place. Since Marcie won't be up and about for a while, I doubt those thugs will return to bother you." I did not want to get into any details about those errands, not with these two ladies.

Thanking them again for the chicken, I slung on my jacket and hat and headed out the back door into the alley. First, I needed to find

Rafe. He had some good contacts on the street who might help me locate Marcie's attackers. That would keep me busy until Wolf got back to me. Working on this situation from two angles would also save me time in the long run.

****

Later that evening

Darkness consumed her mind. She had heard voices and felt a gentle touch on her forehead, but none of it made sense. She felt as if she were floating in water, but gradually, physical sensations returned, bringing pain to various parts of her body. Finally, with great effort, Marcie forced her eyes open, but everything remained foggy and blurred. It took all her strength to lift her right hand to rub her face and eyes to clear the fog, but her arm felt heavy. When she finally lifted her arm, instead of her soft fingers touching her face, there was a clunk as something hard pressed against her hand.

Marcie's other hand moved more easily, and her vision began to clear as she rubbed her face and eyes with her left hand. She was lying in a bed, and from the room's appearance and the feel of wires and tubing across her chest, she understood she was in a hospital. She could now see that her right arm was covered in white, which she assumed was a cast. She realized those were only put on a person when something was broken.

She tried to collect her thoughts, her head resting on the pillow. Slowly, as if a collection of individual photographs passed before her eyes, she started to recollect why she was here. She had been waiting for Joshua to arrive at the restaurant, but he was late. She had gone into the bathroom for a few minutes and heard a loud crash while sitting on the toilet. Jumping off the toilet, she pulled up her pants, retrieved her Glock from its holster on her belt, and then threw open the bathroom door. She was immediately knocked to one side, discharging a round that probably went into the ceiling.

After she landed on her back with her weapon still in her hand, she spotted three men approaching her. She managed to fire two more rounds before they knocked the gun from her hand. Based on the shouting and noises the men made, she was sure she had hit at least one of them. That was the last thing she remembered until she woke up a few moments ago. She had no idea what day it was, but it was time to find out. The nurse call button was within reach on the sheets.

She could not have comprehended what would happen when she pushed that button, but not just a nurse rushed into her room. A once-empty room, except for her, was now crowded with two nurses, a doctor, and her mother and sister, who impatiently remained out of the medical staff's way at the back of the room. They both had smiles on their faces.

****

I knew which shelter Rafe usually used, so I headed there first. They wouldn't let me inside, but if Rafe was present, someone could pass a message to him. The walk took only fifteen minutes, and when I arrived, I saw several homeless folks waiting outside. I didn't see Rafe, but another veteran I only knew as Morgan was leaning against the wall, smoking a cigarette.

Approaching him, I questioned, "Hey there, Morgan. How are things?"

"Doin' good, man. Whatcha doing here? Have they decided to let you back in?"

"Not much chance of that. I'm looking for Rafe. Could you check inside to see if he is here and ask him to come out for me?"

"Sure thing. Let me finish this cancer stick, and then I'll go in. They don't let us smoke inside."

It only took Morgan five minutes before he returned with Rafe in tow. "Hey, brother. What ya need?"

"Come with me a minute, will you? I need a favor."

After we moved to the adjacent alley, I said, "I need your help, Rafe, tracking down those gang members who broke into Marcie's restaurant. I know you know more people on the street than I do. I was hoping you could reach out to some of them who might have IDs on the guys I'm after."

"I can surely give it a try. Do you know anything about them at all?"

"I had a good look at three of them when they first broke into the restaurant. The leader was a white man about six feet tall, with a large gut, a ponytail, and a scraggly beard and mustache. Another one was dark-skinned, I don't know the nationality, skinny, and he acted like a meth addict. The third one was Hispanic, very muscular, and good with a knife. I think they might drive around in a black SUV. That's all I've got."

"That will help me get started. By the way, what have you got in that sack? I see some grease leaking through; it smells like fried chicken. How about sparing a piece? It will be much better than what I will be getting inside."

"I will give you one better. Here are two pieces," I said as I reached inside the bag, pulling out a drumstick and a breast. "It's a couple of days old, but it should be pretty good. It's the least I can do for your help."

"Now that's my man. I might not even need to eat inside with this, but I'll have to hide it from everyone else, or we might cause a riot out here. I'll spread the word and let you know as soon as I hear something. I already know who you're talking about, but I'll wait to confirm it with my brothers."

"Great. Thanks, Rafe." I didn't want to hang around any longer, in case the shelter manager came out and saw me. I shook Rafe's hand, which wasn't holding the chicken, part of which was already stuffed in his mouth, and then headed down the street. As much as I wanted to go back to spend the night at the restaurant, I had a couple of contacts I wanted to touch base with. I knew I would need every bit of help I could get, but I couldn't rely on others and would not put anyone else in danger. I had to do it for myself.

****

After the attending physician completed a series of tests on Marcie, he and the nurses left the room so her family could spend time with her. She seemed to have all her senses about her, so the concussion wasn't too bad. She did, however, have a fractured eye socket, broken nose, three cracked ribs, a bruised kidney, and numerous other less serious injuries. The big question that had been on her mind, because she couldn't remember, was whether she had been raped. The doctor confirmed that she had not been sexually molested or raped. It was a surprise to her and him, as he had certainly expected it to happen. He said someone may have scared them off before they reached that point.

Not remembering much of what had happened, Marcie recalled getting a couple of shots off but didn't know if she had hit anyone. Fran answered her thoughts.

"One police officer indicated there was a small blood trail that led out the back door, so it looks like you hit at least one of them. They still have not found or positively identified them."

Fran's comment made Marcie smile. "Maybe the gunshots scared them off, and they needed to tend to their wounded members. I'm glad I was able to hit at least one of them. I don't remember much else."

"Do you remember who was there to tend to your injuries and call 911, Marcie?" Maxine asked.

"Not at all," she stated with a questioning look.

"Well, Mom and I went back to the restaurant the next day to clean up and found Joshua sleeping there. We told him how upset we were that he didn't do his security duties, which ultimately led to the attack on you. Turns out, one of his good friends was the victim of a hit-and-run, so he was delayed waiting for the ambulance. Before we kicked him out, he admitted to bandaging your head and making you comfortable."

"No one was there when the police arrived?"

"Nope. Joshua said he left before the police got there."

"I forgot to mention that he is avoiding the police or officials. I don't know why yet. He briefly discussed his background a few days ago, but not why he had avoided the police. Well, I'm very thankful he helped until the ambulance got there. He may have been the one who chased my attackers off. They were the same ones that first broke in a few days ago."

Now, seeing Marcie's eyes starting to close, Maxine and Fran realized their visit had tired her out and that she needed some sleep. "We need to get out of here now," Maxine whispered to Fran. "She needs to rest."

Hearing them whispering, Marcie opened her eyes. "Thanks for all your help. I don't know when I can get out of here, but I suspect it won't be for a couple of days at least. If you can take care of the restaurant, I would appreciate it. Please don't bother to open it. I will decide what I will do when I get out of here." With that, her eyelids slowly slid closed, and within seconds, her breathing slowed as she slept.

Quietly slipping out of the room, Fran said, "I'm thinking Marcie is going to feel bad about being unable to feed those families that rely on her cheap meals. Do you think the two of us could open the restaurant at least for one meal a day until she is well enough to continue?"

"I think we could," Maxine responded, "but I hope to persuade her to move out of that neighborhood. I've been worried all along that something like this might happen. I feel guilty for not pushing her harder to change locations. And now this has occurred. We'll see what happens when she comes home. She might have second thoughts about staying there."

"You may be right. We shall see," Fran concluded.

CHAPTER 9

It was three days filled with a whole regimen of additional tests before the doctors released Marcie to go home, strongly advising her to spend at least a week in bed. Her sister, mom, and brother visited her daily. Then her mom and sister took her back to her mom's house, where she lived.

Once settled back in bed, against her objections, Marcie expressed concern that her mother and sister would open the restaurant for only one meal a day, fearing that something like this would happen to them.

"Have you seen any of those guys who attacked me hanging around the place?" she questioned her mom. Marcie had previously provided descriptions of the three men to her mom and sister.

"Not at all. We haven't seen Joshua around either. He helped us clean up that day, then said he had some errands to run and would bang on the back door when he could start spending the night again."

"You failed to tell me he helped you clean up the restaurant. How was he doing?"

"He seemed fine, sweetheart, and he was invaluable."

"Well, I am not staying in this bed for a week. I can still come to help a little bit at the restaurant in a couple of days."

"You need to follow the doctor's orders," her mom emphasized with a strict yet caring tone, pointing a finger at her.

"We'll see. I'm stronger than you think, and I don't feel too bad about it. I also need to find out the court date for those guys. I still plan to testify."

"We think you're just going to cause trouble," Fran said. "They might come after you again, especially if they see you out and about at the restaurant. You need to lay low and let this blow over," she begged.

"Mom, you know what Dad would say to that. He would not want them to get away with what they have done. I'm not going to either."

"But…"

"No buts, Mom. You aren't going to talk me out of it. If I need to take out a small loan to install cameras, I will. But I am staying at that location and will testify on the court date, so save your breath. Both of you!"

Seeing that they would not change Marcie's mind, her mom and sister hugged her, saying they would be back with dinner for her that evening so she wouldn't have to get up to cook. After they left, Marcie flopped back onto her pillows, resigned to being babysat by her family, whether she liked it or not. She had to admit to herself that she appreciated it. Despite her mental toughness, her physical well-being did not match up. She was tired. She looked forward to them returning that evening, but she knew she needed sleep right now. Once she accepted her situation, it only took her seconds to drop off to sleep.

****

It was two days ago that I heard back from Rafe. He couldn't identify the names of Marcie's attackers. Still, he had learned they belonged to a very small neighborhood gang that sold drugs in the area and extorted protection money from local businesses, especially those owned and operated by small, minority families. These minorities were the easiest to target, partly because they had children who could be threatened and partly because some of the families were living in the country illegally. He thought they hung out at an abandoned grocery store and gave me the address. That was all Rafe could find out, but it was enough.

It had been a couple of days since I had visited the restaurant, so I thought I would stop by, hoping to get a good meal and maybe spend the night if Marcie's family did not object. With the plan I had in mind for Marcie's attackers, I didn't want to get too close to Marcie's family. I didn't want them to become more entangled in the conflict than they already were.

I returned to the alley behind the restaurant, where darkness had settled over the city. Not knowing if Fran and Maxine were serving meals yet, I waited until after the regular evening mealtime had concluded before I rapped on the alley door. There was no answer. I rapped once more a little harder, but before I finished, I heard the locks clicking inside, and the door cautiously opened.

"Who's there?"

I recognized Maxine's voice. "It's Joshua."

"Oh. Okay." Maxine pushed the door open further. "I wasn't sure who it was, and I didn't want to let those thugs in accidentally."

"It's good to be cautious. Any chance I could get something to eat and maybe spend the night?"

"You certainly can. We have only been serving one meal a day while Marcie has been in the hospital. Come on in."

As I followed Maxine into the kitchen, I turned and locked the door behind me. When I turned around, Fran walked into the kitchen from the dining area.

"Good evening, Joshua. I heard you were looking for a meal."

"Only if it wouldn't be a problem. I will also spend the night watching over the place if that is all right?"

"No. That's no problem. Also, Marcie just wanted us to thank you for your help that night. And by the way, what have you done that has the police looking for you?"

"Not much. I have committed small thefts, mostly to survive, including stealing food. I don't know why they would have targeted me."

"Well, we will respect your privacy as long as you didn't do something serious, like being a serial killer or something?"

I could see the smiles on both their faces, so I knew they were kidding around a bit. "Nope. Nothing like that."

The next half-hour was spent with them getting me something to eat, me enjoying the lasagna meal they provided, and some small talk. Finally, Fran and Maxine said they needed to take something home for Marcie to eat for dinner since she had been released from the hospital that morning.

"How is she doing, if I may ask?"

"She is still quite sore and tired. The doctor recommended a week of bed rest, but we doubt she will follow those instructions. She'll probably be up and about in a day or two. You can't keep that girl down."

"We tried to talk her into laying low for a while and not to testify, but she is determined to put those guys away and won't listen to us."

"She might not have to worry about the trial. She won't have to testify if they don't appear on the court date."

They looked at each other. "Why wouldn't they show up?"

"Oh, any number of reasons. They don't respect the law or the courts and may remain in hiding until the situation cools down. Who knows?"

I didn't realize that Fran and Maxine could see a hint of a smirk on my face and looked at me quizzically.

"Okay. Enough talk. You two need to get that food home to her. Tell her I said hello and hope she gets better soon."

"We will."

After they departed, I locked the front door behind them and went to see if I could find dessert. I had a horrible sweet tooth that had recently gone unsatisfied. I found some chocolate cake that looked several days old but was still chocolate, which is what mattered. I cut myself a generous piece and slowly ate it, savoring its rich flavor. Even after several days, it was still moist.

Retrieving the cot from the storage closet, I opened it and sat down, leaning back against the wall. Several weeks earlier, I had lifted a cell phone from a careless teenager's backpack. It was my only way to communicate electronically, so I turned it on and opened Google Maps. I was surprised that the teenager hadn't canceled the phone service. While most adults use passwords to lock their phones, I suspected teens often don't bother, which was the case here. I had easy access.

Walking through a dilapidated section of my neighborhood, I looked for the address of the abandoned grocery store that had been partially burned and looted during a riot a couple of years earlier. The owners had moved on, no longer wanting to live or work in the area, fearing the same thing might happen again.

According to Rafe, this gang, which Rafe said had only about eight or ten members, had reportedly fixed up the inside, and they supposedly worked out of the store and slept there. I found some old Google Photos of the place that showed it was still in operation when the pictures were taken. However, the other photos around the area gave me ideas about where I could position myself to watch the place without being seen. Depending on what I discovered, I would plan as I went along.

The store was only four blocks from my current location and was even more rundown than Marcie's restaurant. I would get some sleep, then walk over there in the morning. As I lay back on my cot, I realized it had been a while since I'd experienced those intense headaches. I didn't know why, but I would have such headaches whenever I was very angry or stressed, and I'd been pretty calm lately. Hopefully, the headaches won't return in the next couple of weeks. I'd need all my senses to be sharp, but right now, my main goal is a good night's sleep.

****

Unlocking the front door, Maxine and Fran entered the house, making enough noise that Marcie, if she were awake, would know it was them and not someone breaking in.

"I'm awake, you two," Marcie hollered as she pulled the covers back up after climbing back in bed. She had been sitting in a chair in the front room, but when she saw her family drive up, she would catch hell from them if they had known she wasn't in bed all day.

"We brought you some lasagna," Fran said as her mom continued into the kitchen to heat the meal. "Have you been behaving?"

"Yes, sister. I've just been reading and sleeping." She didn't like lying, but it was for self-preservation. "Did you, by chance, see Joshua tonight?"

"We did. He came looking for a meal and would spend the night."

As Fran entered the room holding a plate of heated lasagna, which she handed to Marcie, she said, "And he asked about you and said he hoped you got well soon. He also said something that we both raised our eyebrows at."

"What was that?"

"He said that if those thugs didn't show up for court, you wouldn't have to testify. He had a strange look when he said that, and we both talked about it in the car, wondering if he was going to do something that might stop them from appearing in court."

"That is interesting. If the police already want him, that won't help his situation. I hope he doesn't do anything to get himself in more trouble."

"We don't know what he meant, but it was just how he said it and the look on his face. We think he is up to something."

"We can't do anything about that. Just pray he stays safe," Marcie stated with a sad look.

"You like him, don't you?" Fran burst out.

"What! No! Well…" Marcie stumbled with her words. "He seems like an okay guy who was dealing with some hard times. I feel bad for him."

"I can see that look in your eyes, young lady," her mom said. "Don't you be getting too involved with him, even if he has helped you out of some bad situations."

"I won't, Mom. Don't worry." But Marcie knew her mom was right. She had started growing fond of Joshua, but deep down, she knew nothing could come of it. Maybe she should check up on him to better understand him. She still had some Marine friends she could contact to research him. That might help her know his thoughts and actions toward her, especially since he hesitated to talk about his deployment to Afghanistan.

"Mom, would you get my laptop from my backpack in the living room? I want to do some stuff on it tonight."

After Marcie finished her dinner and cleaned the dishes, Fran said good night and left for home after giving Marcie a big hug. Along with her mom, they encouraged Marcie to stay in bed, and Marcie assured her she would.

Since it was getting late, Marcie sent her mom to bed, opened her laptop, and began preparing e-mails to Marine friends she knew were still on active duty. She hoped and prayed for good news about Joshua, but she wasn't going to have too high expectations. From what little she knew of him, he probably had a dark side. Only time and research would tell.

CHAPTER 10

In an abandoned Five-and-Dime building, two storefronts down, and across the street from the old grocery store building that the gang used as their operations center, drug den, and sleeping quarters, among other things, was a perfect place where I could conduct my surveillance. The building had a back entry door, and I easily bypassed the rusted lock. What was left of the office looked out onto the street. I could come and go as I pleased, day or night, without being seen by anyone in or around the grocery store.

The refrigerator at Marcie's restaurant provided me with enough food and water to hang out there for several days. I only took items that appeared several days old and would probably be thrown out soon, but it was a feast considering what I could usually scrounge on the street.

On my first day of surveillance, the traffic coming and going from the store mostly looked drug-related. I hadn't seen any of those three gang members I was searching for, and I didn't know what the fourth one looked like. I planned to wait until it got dark, then scout around the store to see if I could either get inside or, at the very least, peek through some windows to spot any of those three men.

Since there were no active restaurants or food sources nearby, nor were there any homeless people on the streets, the vehicle traffic was minimal, and so were the people on foot. I wasn't being picky; I would take on whichever gang member I could hit first. Unfortunately, if they all just lingered around the store, I couldn't pick them off one by one, and I didn't feel like tangling with eight or ten of them at once, especially if they were hyped up on drugs. As I learned in the Marine Corps, patience would be my most valuable tool.

With shadows creeping across the street like an approaching thunderstorm, the area slipped into darkness as the sun quickly sank below the rooftops. The grocery store windows were either boarded up or covered with plastic or other material; I couldn't see any movement inside. Then the door opened with Ponytail—as I had nicknamed the man I thought was the leader of the group—stepping out onto the sidewalk, accompanied by Methhead. Although I couldn't hear what they were saying, it looked like an argument was happening, which was confirmed when I saw Ponytail grab Methhead by the front of his jacket and shout in his face.

Slamming Methhead up against the store's external wall, Ponytail shouted some more, then pushed him down the street, reentering the store. *Finally*, I thought to myself. *One of them alone.* Ensuring I knew which direction Methhead was going, I exited my post out the back door, coming out of the alley onto the street. I observed Methhead stumbling down the street with his arms wrapped around his body like he was cold.

Traveling on the opposite side of the street, I could stay in the shadows and still follow Methhead without being seen. After staggering two blocks, Methhead turned left, heading toward an area I knew had some still-open stores. One was a 24-hour liquor store; I suspected that was where he was headed. Turns out I was right. Three blocks later, Methhead entered an alley, and from my vantage point, I could see him walk twenty or thirty feet down before banging on a back door. When the door opened, Methhead forced his way inside, slamming the door behind him.

Crossing from my side of the street, I entered the alley to find a dumpster surrounded by cardboard liquor boxes, which gave me plenty of concealment. My bad leg screamed at me as I crouched behind the boxes, but I needed to stay out of sight until Methhead exited the store. I prayed he would exit the same way he entered, and I hoped it wouldn't be long, as my leg couldn't stand being in this position for long. I was confident Methhead had entered this store either to get his leader some booze or to collect protection money from the owner or both.

I didn't spend much time in this part of town, even though it wasn't far from where I lived. There wasn't much here for me. I seem to remember that this store was owned by an Indian family who didn't hire anyone outside the family, so the wife and teenage daughter were often in the store, cleaning and helping to stock shelves. That made this store an easy target for a gang like this one.

Before leaving the Five-and-Dime store where I was conducting surveillance, I had thrown a peanut butter and jelly sandwich into my jacket pocket along with a bottle of water. I hadn't had time to eat anything for dinner and didn't know how long I would be away. Pulling both items out of my pocket, I consumed the sandwich in seconds and followed it with half the small water bottle. It was a good thing I did.

The alley door to the liquor store slammed open, and Methhead stepped out into the alley. He had a paper sack in one hand, which seemed to contain one or more bottles of alcohol. His other arm was wrapped around the waist of a teenage Indian girl who, in the store's light, looked frightened and was trying to break free from Methhead's grip. The girl's mother and father stood in the doorway, shouting at Methhead to let their daughter go. Methhead's shouting and profanity in response made the couple cringe in fear against the door frame, their arms wrapped around each other.

Rather than let her go, Methhead bent down, placing the sack on the ground. Then, with one hand around the girl's waist and the other on her breast, he started trying to kiss her and pulled at the hem of her skirt.

The anger started to boil up inside me. Without realizing it, I threw the cardboard boxes aside as I stood up, then rushed across the small alley toward the scene. With my Stetson pulled down and my scarf pulled up over my mouth, my face was mostly hidden so the Indian family wouldn't recognize me. Methhead was so caught up in molesting the teenage girl, along with her parents shouting at him, that he didn't notice the danger behind him. By the time he did, it was already too late.

Reaching down to the sack Methhead had placed on the ground, I quickly wrapped my hand around a bottle's neck, pulled it out of the sack, and struck Methhead across the side of his head. Seeing me approach in the dark alley, the teenage girl's parents suddenly stopped shouting, which caused Methhead's loud scream from the blow to his head to slice through the silence of the alley. Releasing the girl, he fell to his knees, stunned but not unconscious. I pushed the teenager back toward her parents inside the store, then grabbed Methhead's arm, twisting it behind his back before he had a chance to regain his wits.

Wrenching Methhead's arm high behind his back, I felt it dislocate at the shoulder, which elicited another scream from him. As he turned his head toward me, starting to scream again at me this time,

I slammed a fist into his jaw, rendering him unconscious, dropping him on his face to the alley floor. Next, I moved to the liquor store door and slammed it shut, cutting the family off from viewing what I was about to do. Returning to Methhead, I stretched his inert body out on the ground, extending both his arms and hands out flat. Since Methhead was still unconscious, he did not feel the pain or scream as I stomped with my boots on both of his hands, shattering all ten fingers.

Looking around to see if I had drawn anyone's attention and finding I had not, I lifted Methhead onto one shoulder, limped over to the dumpster, threw back the lid, and unceremoniously discarded him into the debris. I then flipped the lid back down. I was sure Methhead would survive, but he wouldn't be useful to anyone for quite a while. Although this gang member might soon be missed when he didn't return to Ponytail with the booze, many things could have happened to him. Ponytail and the rest of his gang probably wouldn't be on alert until someone found Methhead in the dumpster or he managed to climb out. One down and three to go.

****

Marcie had received e-mails from three of her active-duty Marine friends acknowledging her requests and assuring her that they would do their best to answer her questions. They all informed her that it might take a few days, but they would let her know what they found. None of them had asked her why she wanted the information. She felt they instinctively knew she had a good reason, or she wouldn't have asked.

To ensure she got a good night's sleep, Marcie took a couple of sleep aids her doctor had given her. She needed to feel rested the next day because she had a lot she wanted to accomplish despite the doctor's orders. After turning out the light and sliding under the covers, her thoughts drifted back to Joshua. He was a strange person. He was kind but also violent, in great health but sometimes overwhelmed by painful headaches. Yet there was something about him, an unseen force that seemed to draw her to him.

Sometimes, he almost made her heart flutter, but that couldn't be because it hadn't been that many months since she lost her husband, and she loved him dearly. However, there was something different about Joshua, and she felt it that first night when she fed him at the restaurant. Perhaps learning more about his background would explain it.

With that as her last thought, and with a bit of a smile on her face despite the fractured eye socket and broken nose, Marcie slid into sleep.

CHAPTER 11

Intense rays of morning sun pierced through the window where the curtain wasn't fully closed, hitting Marcie right in the face and waking her from her deep sleep. It was almost 8:00 a.m. She knew she needed the sleep, but it was getting late in the morning, and she was wasting time.

Since her injuries, she had moved downstairs into a small extra bedroom so she wouldn't have to climb the stairs to her usual room. As she swung her legs out from under the covers and her feet hit the floor, she heard her mom in the kitchen, followed by the doorbell ringing. *I wonder who that could be this early,* she thought. Then she recognized her brother's deep voice and listened as his wheelchair rolled across the floor. The banging on her bedroom door was him letting her know it was time to get up.

Padding barefoot across the floor, she opened the door and grinned down at him. Even though he could be irritating at times, she could never stay mad at him. Although they weren't twins, their bond felt just as close. For as long as she could remember, they had been nearly inseparable, but the events of 9/11 changed that. John had insisted on enlisting in the Marines. Marcie knew she would also enlist, but she hesitated because of pressure from her mom and sister. After her enlistment and training, she and her brother managed to find times to visit each other while both were overseas, but they had never been assigned to the same unit.

The IED that destroyed the Humvee he was driving that fateful day and caused his injuries devastated her, but the brother/sister bond they shared helped him recover and also supported her in coping with nearly losing him.

"Morning, sis," John said as Marcie leaned down to hug and kiss him. "Being a sleepyhead, I see."

"Don't give me any trouble. I'm just following the doctor's orders. Get some breakfast from Mom. I'll be out in a minute." It was good to see him in such a good mood. On rare occasions, he would fall into a mild depression, but she could usually bring him out of it, just like he could lift her out of feeling sad for herself.

Throwing on some jeans with holes in the knees and a Marine sweatshirt, Marcie slipped her feet into slippers, then carefully headed into the bathroom to fix her hair and face. It was more difficult than usual because every time she lifted her arms above her shoulders, her injured ribs protested loudly. Finally, satisfied she looked good enough for her family, she moved into the kitchen.

A plate of food was already on the table for her, and her brother was already digging into his breakfast, not waiting for her. "Boy, what respect. Not even waiting for me. Did you say your prayers first, I hope?" she asked as she grabbed him around the shoulders.

"Uh… yeah, I did."

She looked at her mom, who had a questioning expression. "What? To yourself? My little brother. You may not think the Lord was watching over you when that IED went off, but He kept you alive, and with the help of your brothers gin arms, He brought you back to us. Remember that every time you forget to pray and thank Him for all you have."

"I know. I know. I have some trouble with it sometimes."

"Whether you realize it or not, John, you have a guardian angel watching over you, just like Mom and I do. Mine took the form of Joshua a couple of times already."

"Who's Joshua?"

"I told you about the homeless man who helped me when those gang members broke in and tried to rob me."

"Yes, but you never mentioned his name. Is he also the one who helped you when you ended up in the hospital?"

"Yes. Mom and Fran asked him about that the other night, and he confirmed it was him, but he left before any help arrived. For some reason, he doesn't want any contact with the police, so I haven't mentioned him to them. He was also a Marine."

"Really, where was he stationed?"

"I don't know. He told me he was in Afghanistan, but didn't talk much about that. He has a bad leg and gets severe headaches. He also has PTSD and anger issues. Those issues have made him *persona non grata* at all the shelters around. He is too disruptive, so I have been helping him a bit."

"So, next time you see him, try to find out what unit he was assigned to. Maybe we had mutual friends."

"I will ask, but he's not talkative about his military time. It almost seems like a bad trip for him, and he doesn't want to relive it. Mom and Fran said he hasn't been around the restaurant lately. He told them he had some errands to take care of."

John paused as he wheeled his chair from the kitchen through the living room and headed toward the bathroom. Sensing movement, he looked out the living room window and observed a police car pulling up. "Looks like we have company, Marcie."

After approaching the front door, Marcie opened it just as Officer Duncan was about to knock. "Good morning, Officer. This is a surprise visit. Are you still trying to ask me out? If so, the answer is still no."

He responded, looking somewhat embarrassed, as that was probably exactly what was on his mind, "No, I am here strictly on business. Have you had any contact with any of those individuals who assaulted you?"

"No, not at all. Why do you ask?"

"Something strange happened last night. One of them was caught trying to climb out of a dumpster. He was in bad shape. He had a dislocated shoulder, and both hands and all his fingers were broken. Shattered might be a better description. Do you know anything about that?"

"What a stupid question. I just got out of the hospital last night and have been home recovering."

"It turns out we questioned the owners of a liquor store near that alley, and they said this same injured man entered their store last night, stole money out of their register, took two bottles of liquor, and then started molesting their daughter. They said as this guy pulled their daughter into the alley, someone came out of the darkness and attacked the molester. They didn't see what happened after that because he pushed their daughter back into their store and slammed the door shut."

Standing in astonishment, Marcie wasn't sure whether to ask any questions, but finally did. "What did the person who rescued their daughter look like?"

"Why, do you know who did it?"

"Of course not. I just wondered if it was some homeless person who was trying to right a wrong."

"The store owners didn't get a good look at the person. They said he appeared to be a large man with a big, wide-brimmed hat pulled down over his eyes and a scarf wrapped around his face."

Not wanting to let Officer Duncan see the recognition on her face, Marcie rapidly turned toward her mom and brother, asking, "You two don't know anything about this, do you?"

Seeing the look in Marcie's eyes, they both denied knowing anything about the incident or who might have attacked the thief, but Maxine said, "Well, whoever it was, it served the punk right. Now he knows what it's like. Is he still alive?"

"He is, but he isn't going to hurt anyone anytime soon. He can't even feed himself with his hands because they're so messed up. I just wanted to tell you what happened and see if you have any leads. No matter what he did to you, Marcie, I don't think he deserved what happened."

"I will feel a little better knowing he is off the street. If you have no further questions, my breakfast is getting cold." Marcie had composed herself and kept a straight face as she saw Duncan off. As he turned back toward her, before he could say a word, she said, "And the answer is still no. I won't go out with you. Good day."

Retreating into the kitchen, Marcie saw her mom standing with her hands on her hips and her brother just looking at her. Maxine was the first to speak. "That was Joshua, wasn't it? The description fit him down to the hat and scarf."

"Perhaps. But we can't be positive, and I wasn't going to give him up to the police, regardless of suspecting he attacked that creep for me. Maybe for that young girl, but for me too."

After reheating her cooled-down breakfast in the microwave, Marcie sat back down. Looking at her brother and mom, she said, "No further talk about this. Got it?"

Both ran their fingers across their lips as if closing zippers. Then they returned to the kitchen table to finish their breakfast. Marcie immediately started spearing food into her mouth, which was the only way she could keep the grin that kept trying to spread across her face from turning into an actual smile.

****

I had a pretty good night's sleep in my newly found auto repair shelter. The knuckles on my right hand were a little bruised from when I hit Methhead to silence him, but other than that, I felt good. It was time to head back to the Five-and-Dime hideout to keep watch on the gang's activities. I wouldn't say I enjoyed wandering those streets during daylight hours, but it wasn't much of a walk from where I was. If I took my time and just shuffled along, I shouldn't draw anyone's attention. I was eager to find out how Marcie was doing, but that would have to wait for another time.

Although I stayed on the shaded side of the street, away from the sunny side where most people experiencing homelessness gathered to enjoy the warm sun, I still recognized several people I knew, or at least remembered. I had some extra fruit in the pockets of my heavy jacket, so since I had a relatively steady supply of good food if I wanted it, I shared the fruit.

Despite the delays, I arrived at my Five-and-Dime store across from the gang headquarters in half an hour. Jiggling the rusted lock, it popped open, giving me easy access to the store. It still looked like I had this place to myself.

Moving to a front window with a better view, I tore small holes in the paper covering the windows and then looked through them at the abandoned grocery store across the street. I saw no activity, which wasn't surprising since these gangbangers probably worked best in the dark; they were likely lying low and resting until evening. I pulled a desk chair up to the window, making it easier to watch the street. I would need some rest if I had to go out again tonight, which is when I did my best work.

CHAPTER 12

Marcie's mother, sister, and brother managed to keep her at home for another day. Although she didn't always stay in bed, she was at least taking it easy, avoiding lifting anything or doing any work. She was antsy and wanted to go back to the restaurant, but her family had teamed up against her. Of course, since they took her car keys away, she was stuck at home.

Finally, after three days, she convinced them she was well enough to return to the restaurant, as long as she promised to let her mom and sister handle the heavy work. Her face was still black and blue, and no amount of makeup could fully hide the bruises. This morning, her mom was already outside warming up the car, while Marcie put on her coat and then her warm, fur-lined gloves. She heard her laptop, which she was carrying to work, ding, indicating she had an email. She thought about stopping to check the email, but didn't want to keep her mom waiting, so she kept going out the door and locked it behind her. She could check her email at the restaurant.

Fran had already arrived and was preparing breakfast. They had switched to two meals a day, now serving an early breakfast and a late lunch, which many patrons often used as dinner.

Marcie slipped out of her coat and gloves, threw them over one of the bench seats, grabbed a cup of hot black coffee, and then cautiously slid into the seat, flipping open her laptop. Several emails appeared on her screen. Most of them were about work or from friends asking how she was doing, but one stood out. It was from her 1st Sgt., who had tried to persuade her to stay in the Marine Corps rather than take her honorable discharge for humanitarian reasons after her husband was killed.

She opened the email that had arrived several days earlier and found limited information about Joshua, but enough to answer some questions. He was assigned to the 2nd Battalion, 24th Marines in Fallujah and had been seriously wounded there, which led to his medical discharge. The email also informed her that the 1st Sgt. had a close friend and comrade in Washington who might provide him with more details.

Just as she was about to close her computer to help her mom and sister with breakfast preparations, it dinged again. It was another email from the same 1st Sgt. Her mouth dropped open as she read the message, surprised and confused. The part that stood out was that Sgt. Joshua Gibbs had been awarded the Medal of Honor for his actions in Fallujah, which saved several of his comrades and left him with multiple injuries. A note at the bottom explained that this was a very unusual situation, as Joshua's father had also received the Medal of Honor for his actions during the Vietnam War. There had been only two previous instances in which a father and son both received the award. Her 1st Sgt. noted that Joshua had dropped off the radar after returning to the States and being discharged.

Marcie needed to speak with her brother. Could Joshua possibly be the person who saved him? What kind of coincidence would that be? But how did he end up homeless on the streets? Deciding she would stay until after closing in hopes of Joshua returning to the restaurant for a meal or a place to sleep, she closed her computer and left the booth to greet some customers she knew but hadn't seen in a while. It would be hard waiting until closing, but perhaps the time would pass quickly if she kept busy.

****

The only activity I noticed during the day was Ponytail stepping outside the store where the gang was hiding, looking up and down the street. Even though I couldn't read lips, it looked like he was cursing a blue streak. Ponytail probably didn't care much about Methhead, but it was the money and booze he was after.

With no further action that could help me, I decided to call off my watch and get some sleep. I will try again tomorrow. As I climbed into a more comfortable chair than the desk chair I had been sitting in most of the day, I heard a noise at the back of the building. Sliding out of the chair, I went to the back door. I could hear the door rattling as someone tried to pry it open.

The deadbolt I used to lock the door each time I entered was still sturdy and rust-free. If someone was determined and had the right tool, they might be able to open it. I couldn't risk anyone discovering what I was doing, so I had to scare them off.

"Get out of here. This place is occupied!" My deep, booming voice echoed inside the empty building. I then banged on the wall to make sure I had scared the person away. Standing quietly for several minutes and hearing no further noise, I felt I could return to my lounge chair. When I got up in the morning, I might need to find a better lock for the outside to secure this opening so no one could gain entry while I was gone. Fortunately, there was a working toilet in a small bathroom off the main store floor, so I didn't have to search for another place to take care of my daily business.

As I climbed back onto my recliner, an intense migraine headache slammed behind my eyes as if someone had hit me with a baseball bat. Curling up in the recliner with my head tightly in my hands, tears welled up from the pain. The urge to scream rumbled in my throat, but then the pain and stress caused me to lose consciousness once again. It never lasted long, but I couldn't do anything to stop it.

****

Marcie was pleased to see many familiar faces of the families she had fed for months. Most of them approached her, asking about her health and expressing gratitude that she was okay and the restaurant was open. None of the customers mentioned the bruises on her face. The friendship of these families helped the day pass quickly, and Marcie realized it was time to close. They had closed several hours earlier, but there was always plenty of work to clean up and get ready for the next day.

Marcie knew she would stretch out her cleanup work in hopes that Joshua would show up, but it was now getting late, and there was still no sign of him. Her sister had already left, and her mom was ready to leave as well, and she was her ride back to the house. Frustrated, she grabbed her coat and gloves, motioned to her mom, and said she was ready to leave. They both departed through the front door, locking it behind them. Marcie was hyperalert to anyone else on the street and was hyperaware of anything that seemed out of place. Her Glock had been stolen when she was attacked in the restaurant, and she did not have the money to replace it. Seeing no one, they climbed into her mom's car and drove down the street, with Marcie glancing in the rearview mirror, hoping to catch a glimpse of Joshua. There was no such luck.

The next morning, as the sun broke through low-hanging clouds hinting at rain or snow, Marcie turned over in bed, realizing she wasn't feeling well. She felt her forehead, shivered from a chill, and knew she had a fever. She understood she might have an infection from one of her many cuts or scrapes from her attack, but she'd been taking antibiotics and thought she'd be okay. However, based on how she felt that morning, that wasn't the case.

The bedroom door opened, and her mom was standing there. "Are you going to get up, lazyhead?"

"Don't think so, Mom. I'm not feeling so good this morning."

"What's the matter?" she questioned, coming over to the bed and sitting on its edge.

"I've got some chills and fever. I may have an infection somewhere."

Feeling Marcie's forehead, she confirmed her assessment and said she would call the doctor. A few minutes later, Maxine returned to Marcie's room and told her that the doctor wanted her to come in to see him sooner rather than later.

"I will call Fran and tell her we won't be in for a while and not to open the restaurant if she doesn't think she can handle it."

"I hate to do that, Mom. So many people rely on us. Why don't you drop me off at the doctor's office, and then you can go on to help Fran? I can catch a cab to the restaurant when I am finished or come home."

Having agreed with Marcie's suggestion, Maxine bundled her up, got her into the car, and headed to the doctor. When Maxine arrived at the restaurant, Fran was already cooking and serving families, so she didn't waste time shedding her coat, putting on an apron, and relieving Fran of cooking so she could serve the customers.

Maxine's phone rang two hours later, and Marcie told her she was back home with a stronger antibiotic. The doctor didn't know the cause of the fever, but he increased the antibiotic because Marcie's immune system was weakened. He also advised her to eat plenty of plain yogurt to counteract the effects of the antibiotics, which kill both good and bad bacteria. Marcie had learned to like the unflavored yogurt abroad and even developed a taste for the yogurt drink called Ayran. The doctor told Marcie to call back in four days if she wasn't feeling better.

****

Although I didn't plan to stay overnight at the restaurant, I needed some good food. I had exhausted the supplies I stole there the last time I visited. I wasn't sure if Marcie would come back to work, but I hoped to see her while I was there.

When I reached the alley door of the restaurant, I only had to wait a few seconds, knocking until it opened, with Fran standing there. "Good evening, young lady. Can a poor homeless person get a meal here?"

"Well, hello, Joshua. We haven't seen you in a few days. How are you? And of course, you can get a meal. Marcie is not here, however. She was okay yesterday, but she came down with a fever this morning. Mom took her to the doctor, and she is back home now.

Come on in. We are about ready to leave. Are you going to spend the night?"

I could sense Fran's relaxed nature and was thrilled that she and her mom had accepted me despite my current situation. The headache attack I had the night before had really left me drained, and I hadn't felt like eating anything all day, but now I was starving.

"I have another place I have been staying, but if you want me to watch over the place tonight, I can do that."

I thought it would help me gather some extra food to stockpile at my observation post so I wouldn't have to go out as much and could spend more time watching the gang.

"Make yourself at home, then. We are headed out of here." As Fran turned to leave with her coat on, she stopped and turned back to me. "By the way, you might have heard. One of those gang members who assaulted Marcie was found all beaten up in a dumpster a couple of nights ago. I don't suppose that was one of the little errands you had to take care of, was it?"

"I hadn't heard that, Fran." I disliked lying, but I cannot involve these women in my crimes. Then I added, "Serves him right. I wish I could have been the one to give him a beating. If you ever find out who did it, thank him for me."

As Fran turned to leave with her mother, I added, "Please tell Marcie hi for me. I hope she gets better."

****

They acknowledged they would pass my message on to her and left the restaurant. I locked it behind them, then returned to the kitchen to set up my cot. I would probably leave before they came back in the morning so I could get the food out. I wasn't planning to take anything they could serve to customers, just items that looked several days old or that they might be about to throw away. From conversations I had with the women over the past few weeks, I had heard that Marcie wasn't doing well financially, and I didn't want to take anything that could help fill her cash register.

After eating a meal of heated spaghetti and bread, I lay down on my cot. I needed to come up with another plan to reach the other gang members. I had only caught glimpses of Ponytail and the Hispanic guy I nicknamed Jose, but no opportunity arose to follow either of them. I still didn't know who the fourth gang member was—he was the one who hit me on the head. It seemed all the gang members stayed close to their building. As I drifted off to sleep, I considered checking out the area next to or behind the grocery store where the gang was based to see if I could get better access. If I could do that, maybe I could position myself to listen in on what was happening there. That might help me come up with a better plan.

****

Marcie greeted Fran and her mom at the door when they arrived home from the restaurant. "How did it go today? Did you see Joshua?"

"First, what are you doing up? You should be in bed."

"I am feeling a bit better already. Did you see Joshua?"

"Why is that so important? But to answer your question, yes, we did, and he said to say hello. He was going to spend the night in the restaurant."

"Dang. I missed him. There was something I wanted to discuss with him. Is he going to be there in the morning?"

"Don't know. Now, what is so important that you must be out of bed?"

Walking over to sit on the couch, Marcie said, "I just found out some information about him and where he was assigned in Afghanistan. I wanted to discuss that with him. That's all." Marcie didn't want to reveal the information until she had gathered more details. It was probably all for nothing. It was unlikely that Joshua was connected in any way with her brother's injuries, but if there was even a slight chance, she wanted to explore it.

Marcie suddenly realized how late it was and how tired she felt, so she said good night to her mom and sister and went to bed. If she felt like it, she would try to visit the restaurant in the morning, hoping Joshua would still be there.

CHAPTER 13

I was awake before sunrise with my pockets and a small bag loaded with food. I had enough to last several days, even though I thought completing my mission wouldn't take long. I hoped it wouldn't. Leaving the restaurant this early reduced the risk of running into Marcie and having to answer questions, especially about what I was doing, particularly if it involved lying to her or her family. The medications I used to control my PTSD and headaches were running low, so I needed to find a way to get more, hopefully without going to a doctor. There were a couple of sources I could contact if Rafe or Wolf couldn't get me what I needed.

Although I still had enough for a couple of days, if I didn't get my meds soon, I would be in for a world of hurt. To return to my Five-and-Dime observation post, I took my typical back street and alley route. I knew I should probably check on my other location at the auto repair place to make sure no one else had taken it over, but my priority was to keep a close eye on the gang.

Over the past week or so, the weather had remained fairly mild, but this morning the temperature dropped several degrees, and some ominous clouds moved in to cover the city. Although the Seattle area usually doesn't get much snow, there's always an exceptional year. I prayed the snow would stay away because if it didn't, I'd leave footprints everywhere I went, especially if I tried to get closer to the gang's office across the street.

The snow didn't hold off, but it was not cold enough to stick to the ground. Instead, it just turned every place I walked into a slushy mess. I suspected the snow would melt entirely by the end of the day, which would greatly please me.

It was almost noon when I noticed any movement around the abandoned grocery store. First, two people came out of the front door. I didn't recognize them, but one might have been the fourth gang member who hit me on the head that first night at Marcie's restaurant. He had a bandage on his leg and was walking with crutches. I remembered either Fran or Maxine—I couldn't recall which—mentioning that Marcie had fired a couple of shots when she was attacked, and the police told them there was a blood trail outside the door. The man leaned against the wall with the other person while Ponytail joined them. All three stood and talked for a few seconds, then Ponytail went back inside with the other two, trudging down the street through the two or three inches of slushy snow with unhappy looks. On a day like this, they probably thought they could stay warm and dry inside.

It wasn't that I couldn't handle two gang members at one time, especially with one being injured, but it certainly raised the risk, and if I slipped up the least little bit, it could be a problem. I noticed the two gang members were heading in the same direction Methhead had gone, so I wondered if they were going to the same liquor store to look for information about Methhead.

Anticipating they might also be prone to violence with the Indian family if they didn't get the information they wanted, I decided I needed to keep a close watch on them to prevent anything from happening. If I could also neutralize these two, that would be two fewer gang members I would have to deal with.

Exiting the Five-and-Dime alley door, it only took me a couple of minutes to see the two I would follow. Not many people were on the street—homeless or otherwise—in this kind of weather, but I still had to be cautious and avoid being spotted. Within fifteen minutes, I determined I was right; they were headed to the liquor store. It looked like they were going in the front door, so I moved into the alley in hopes they would exit the alley door.

Just as I positioned myself next to the same dumpster where I had hidden the last time I was here, a police car slowed down at the alley's entrance. There was little light in the alley, and at first, I didn't think the officers could see me, but when they turned on their red and blue flashing light bar and one officer exited the car heading my way, I knew I was in trouble.

Fortunately, the police's arrival may have kept the two gang members from causing trouble, as one officer stayed in the car parked almost directly across the street from the liquor store. As I bolted from my hiding spot, stumbling into and knocking over cardboard boxes, I heard the officer shout at me to stop. Knowing that if I stopped, they would identify me and I would be in serious trouble, I ran as fast as my injured leg allowed.

After just a few yards down the alley, I heard a door slam open. Glancing over my shoulder, I saw two men rushing out of the liquor store into the alley and crashing into a police officer. The officer was propelled into the alley wall, collapsing among a pile of boxes. The two men were now running behind me like crazy and would soon catch up if I didn't act fast.

There was no way, with my bad leg, that I was going to outrun the two men, so the only thing I could do was dive behind another dumpster at the other end of the alley and hope they would pass me by in their attempt to escape the police. It worked. I didn't know what they had been doing in the liquor store, but they now seemed only interested in saving themselves and hardly even looked at my huddled, curled-up form behind the dumpster.

Once the two men passed and turned left onto the street, which would take them back to their grocery store, I got up, headed out to the street, and turned right to avoid any further contact with them. Now was not the time to cause any issues, especially with the police so close. I would have to wait for another day.

****

Marcie tried every trick and rationalization she could think of to persuade her mom and sister to let her go to the restaurant with them, but it was to no avail. They weren't going to give in. So, she resigned herself to spending another day at home. She could use that time to call her brother and ask him to come over to discuss the information she had learned about Joshua. It might clear up everything bouncing around in her head, or it might not.

It took Marcie half the day to finally reach John, but he was being fitted with his leg prosthetics at the physical therapist's office, so he couldn't come over to the house. She didn't want to discuss Joshua with him over the phone, so she agreed to stay home the next day when he was available to visit.

As Marcie walked into the kitchen to make tea, she noticed the calendar on the wall. It was circled in red around the next day's date with the note "Court." She had become so absorbed in everything related to Joshua that she completely forgot tomorrow was the first court date for her attackers. She was surprised that she hadn't been contacted by the DA's office regarding her preparation to testify.

Maybe the first day or two were reserved for motions, jury selection (if applicable), or other administrative procedures.

After Marcie found the courthouse phone number, she spent the rest of the afternoon shuffling from person to person, trying to determine her responsibilities and when she would be needed. She finally learned that the defendants would make a plea deal, and her testimony might not even be required. She was livid, shouting out her anger at whoever she was talking to at the time, and then she slammed the phone on the table. That seemed to be the way of this city: to punish criminals in the smallest possible amount of time, so there was time to address the more serious crimes. Well, in her mind, the crimes against her were serious, but she didn't know what she could do to change anything.

Stumbling into her bedroom and falling on her back onto the bed, she lay there sobbing until the effort wore her out, and she slipped off into sleep. She didn't hear her mother and sister return from the restaurant, but when she woke up the following day, a blanket was thrown across her, and her slippers were off, lying by the side of the bed.

She recalled the previous day's phone calls and the conclusions she had drawn as she threw the blanket back and stepped into her slippers. Although she wasn't happy about the probable outcome, she resigned herself to not letting it get her down and returned to work. People needed her; she could not expect her mom and sister to do everything.

She found the coffee in the kitchen hot, but her mom had already gone to the restaurant. Looking out the front window, she saw her sister's car parked in the driveway, so they probably went together in her mom's car. Rummaging around the kitchen, she discovered her sister's car keys on the dining room table. She wasn't sure if her sister had left them there by mistake or if she had intended to give Marcie a car in case she wanted to drive to the restaurant.

It only took her seconds to decide to go to the restaurant, but she needed a shower and clean clothes. Her coffee and breakfast would have to wait.

****

I was getting anxious. Another day in my Five-and-Dime hideout, watching the gang headquarters, was testing my nerves. I was a person of action, and sitting here wouldn't get me anywhere. A decision had to be made: go to the restaurant to try and see Marcie or keep tailing Ponytail and his gang. If I remember right, there was a court date coming up soon, and I didn't want these criminals to slip away. Since most of these gang members were probably armed, it put me at a big disadvantage. On the other hand, carrying a gun of any kind might lead me to do something I'd regret forever. No. I had to be methodical and handle these punks with care.

As darkness fell on the city, ominous clouds covered the sky, blocking out the moon and stars, though in town, too many lights made it impossible to see any stars. The rain started pouring when I stepped out of the alley door into the back alley of my Five-and-Dime. At first, it was just a drizzle, but it gradually turned into a heavy downpour. If I stayed outside without cover, I would be soaked through. However, I doubted any gang members would be out tonight, so despite the rain, it was time to sneak closer to their hangout and scout the area.

Except for a siren in the distance, the street was completely quiet. Only the rain hitting metal trash cans or rooftops produced musical notes. No one was on the street, and no cars were passing through. This freedom of movement was essential for my scouting trip.

Even though I was getting wetter by the minute, I took a roundabout route to cross the street and head into the alley behind the grocery store. I didn't know what businesses had previously occupied the storefronts next to the grocery, but I was about to find out. Carefully slipping down the alley, avoiding debris or trash cans that might give me away, I found no alley doors for either of the closed businesses on each side of the grocery. That created a problem for me. I could try to get in through the front of each building, but then I would be visible to passersby, including one of the gang members if he decided to step outside onto the sidewalk.

I found an alley door just one business away from the grocery store. The door was in rough shape, so I used a piece of iron I found behind a dumpster as a pry bar and quickly forced the lock, swinging the door open. I skillfully caught the door before it slammed against the wall. Inside, I recognized that this place had previously been a hair and nail salon. Although the exterior walls were brick, I hoped the interior walls would be framed with two-by-fours and covered with drywall (also known as sheetrock). That would have made it easier to access the neighboring business. Unfortunately, I was out of luck.

As I cut through the sheetrock, I realized it only covered the brick wall that was built when this block's structure was originally erected. *Decision-making time*, I thought to myself. I could try the building on the other side of the grocery, but the odds were that the wall would be the same as this one. My only other option was to attempt chipping through the brick.

Returning to the alley, I picked up the iron bar I had used to pry open the alley door and headed back to the brick wall. First, I tore more sheetrock off the brick to create a larger work area. It seemed over the decades that this brick wall had stood here, at some point, the roof had leaked, allowing water to seep down the wall, eroding the mortar that sealed the bricks together. As I tapped the concrete between the bricks, it flaked and crumbled onto the floor fairly quickly. Within minutes, I had already loosened and removed one brick.

Some of the concrete was more eroded in places than others. Still, an hour later, I had removed enough bricks to allow me easy access to enter the adjoining business once I carefully knocked the sheetrock loose on the other side. I discovered that this business used to be a sewing and fabric store. My stealth had to be even more careful as I entered a room adjacent to the gang headquarters. I had no idea where the adjoining wall connected to the grocery store. It could be adjoining their bedrooms, living area, or kitchen. The gang could have completed many remodeling projects to make the grocery habitable, so I had to move cautiously.

Two things happened while I was removing some of the sheetrock on my side of the wall to expose the brick. First, I found no brick; instead, I was looking at the space between two-by-fours and sheetrock on the other side. Second, I could hear loud voices and shouting coming from behind the wall I was working on. In case they heard me trying to access their area, I crept back to the far side of the room, through the hole into the hair salon, then squatted by the alley door and waited. It was not a matter of fight or flight. I would have run if I had been discovered.

CHAPTER 14

When Marcie arrived at the restaurant, her mother and sister weren't surprised to see her. Her mom poured her a cup of coffee, and they sat in a booth while Marcie explained her efforts from the day before to contact someone in court to find out when she needed to appear to testify. They both groaned when Marcie finished. Maxine and Fran then spent the next hour waiting on customers, cooking, and trying to convince Marcie to close this restaurant and open another one in a safer location. Marcie refused. They eventually left her alone, so she went into the kitchen and sat at a small desk with a computer and printer.

After several minutes, she reentered the dining area and headed to the front windows with some documents. Maxine and Fran followed her.

"What are you doing, Marcie? What is that in your hand?"

"Since I can't afford a security camera system, I can at least cause anyone wanting to cause trouble to have second thoughts."

After taping the papers inside the front windows, she stepped outside with her mom and sister close behind her. Marcie stood back from the window where signs reading "Video Surveillance on the Premises" were taped in two places.

"I guess that might work for a while," Fran said, "but I wouldn't hold my breath that those signs will keep the gang members from coming back here."

"Well, that's all I can do for now. I will contact the bank to see if they will give me a small camera loan. I think it will be worth it if I use a little from my retirement fund. I also need another weapon since they stole mine when they attacked me. If you keep things going for me here, I'll see you back home." Marcie had decided that action on her part was the only way to prevent falling into a well of depression, so action was what she was going to take. Getting into her sister's car, she drove down the street, making her next stop at the bank.

****

The shouting had quieted a bit, and I decided I was no longer the center of their attention. Moving away from the alley door, I crawled back through the hole in the brick wall and approached the shared fabric store wall again. Instead of trying to make a pinhole in the center of the wall, I decided to go down towards the floor and make a small hole in the corner, where it would be less noticeable. I had to move very slowly, not knowing what or who was on the other side of the wall. The fabric store I visited had leftover fabric and a couple of racks stacked with several skeins of yarn. Where there was yarn, there were sure to be knitting needles. It only took me a few minutes to open a drawer and find several different-sized needles.

After carefully removing a square area of sheetrock, about a foot on each side, near the floor on my side of the wall, I slowly started pushing the darning needle through the opposing sheetrock. I knew it was a considerable risk, but I was getting impatient and needed to do this for my peace of mind. Pulling the needle back out, I reclined on my stomach, getting my eye as close to the hole as I could. It was barely a quarter of an inch in diameter, giving me a little view inside the adjoining room.

At first, all I could see was white a few inches from my eye, but the smell that drifted through the hole immediately told me I was looking at the side of a toilet. The nearly overwhelming odor also indicated that the gang members probably didn't use this toilet, which was likely clogged and non-functional. If I could handle the smell, this room might give me access to the gang headquarters. Most stores have men's and women's bathrooms, so I guessed they were using the other one and probably never entered this one because of the smell. Finally, a bit of luck, if I could call it that.

Searching through the fabric store, I finally found a pair of scissors. I needed a sharp edge to cut the sheetrock as quietly as possible. I knew the two-by-fours framing the wall were probably on standard sixteen-inch centers, and I thought I could squeeze between them once the sheetrock was removed. Cutting one of the two-by-fours would be too time-consuming and noisy.

As I finished cutting through the sheetrock on my side of the wall, I pushed the large piece aside in case I needed to exit quickly. I didn't want anything blocking my escape. Now, I moved to the sheetrock on the bathroom side. I cut small sections at a time to remove them quietly and avoid banging them into anything.

After removing the first square foot section, I peeked into the bathroom and confirmed it was a badly clogged toilet. I had smelled worse in Afghanistan, especially when they burned human waste. It took me another half hour to clear enough debris to make access to the bathroom easier. Luckily, the sewage hadn't spilled onto the floor, so I didn't have to walk in it and track it back to where I had been when I left.

While working on the wall, I heard loud music, along with laughter and shouts, coming from the central part of the grocery store. Just as I stepped into the bathroom, I heard a door open and shut nearby, and I froze. The next sounds I heard were water splashing, followed by a toilet flushing. The other toilet must be right next to this one. The other door opened and shut again.

Cautiously listening at the door, I couldn't hear much over the loud music. After about five minutes, someone shouted, "Hey, turn that garbage off while we are trying to conduct business over here." The music ceased, and now I could hear the discussions.

"We're supposed to be in court tomorrow, boss. What are we gonna do?"

"We ain't gonna do nothing. The cops don't know where we are, so we'll sit tight."

"Okay, but we're running low on food. Can't one of us hit the market and resupply?"

"Yeah, but only after it gets dark. And stay away from any populated place. There is a small market located on 68th. Go there, and don't forget the beer."

"Can I take someone with me to help carry stuff?"

"No! Just you. I don't want any more people disappearing on me. Get there and get back here and watch for the cops."

"It's not dark yet. You said wait until it was dark."

"Of course, you idiot."

I then heard a loud slap and a heavy thump on the floor, as if someone had fallen.

"Go get some darker clothes and take that duffel bag with you. Now get outta my sight."

I had heard enough. One gang member was about to leave, and I planned to get to the store before him. That would be one less gang member I had to worry about. It didn't matter if he was one of the ones who assaulted Marcie. I would take them all down if it meant getting them off the streets and delivering some justice for her, which the courts were unlikely to do.

Sneaking back through the hole in the wall, I prayed that none of the gang members would open the bathroom door and catch me in the act of demolishing. When I return, I will need to be careful not to fall into any traps they might set. For now, though, I'm headed to the 68th Street market to see if I can take out another gang member. I have plenty of time, with a few hours before darkness covers the city. The rain has eased up, so I should stay reasonably dry.

The small market on 68th was a few blocks away, and while en route, I stayed in alleys or on empty side streets. I suspected the market had an alley door leading to a dumpster for discarding old food and trash. I was right. As I entered the alley behind the market, I saw a large green dumpster against the wall across from the market, and there was what looked like a steel door that would let me into the market.

Not knowing whether the unknown gang member would come into the market as a regular customer or try to enter through the alley door made me uneasy. From my spot by the dumpster, I could watch the alley door but not see the front door of the market. At any spot on 68th Street, I couldn't effectively monitor the alley door.

Finally, I decided to cross the street into the opposite alley, which would give me a view of the market's front door. I could also tell if someone attempted to enter the store through the alley door. Crossing the street, I found another dumpster to give me a modicum of concealment. I figured I had just over an hour to wait until darkness, but I didn't know how long before the gang member showed up. It was time to be patient.

I awoke with a start. I didn't know what woke me. It may have been a cat or some other furry animal scavenging for food. I didn't realize I had dozed off, but I now observed the alley was dark, and only one dim streetlight scarcely lit up the area. Although I didn't see anyone on the street, it was time to stay awake.

My wait was brief. Several people entered and exited the market across the street, usually women and a few teenage boys. I didn't see anyone who looked like the gang member I was expecting. But coming down the street into the glow of the streetlight, a likely candidate strolled by. He was dressed entirely in black, with a hoodie pulled over his head and his hands shoved in his pockets. Over his shoulder was what looked like a duffel bag, and I remembered the gang leader had told his member to bring one to hold the supplies.

I decided to let the gang member enter the store, grab his food, and then leave unless he started hurting someone inside. He would be an easier target once he returned to his headquarters loaded down.

I noticed another alley a block away, in the same direction the gang member had come. It would be the perfect spot to wait and catch him as he lumbered by, loaded down with food. No lit storefronts were on my side of the street, so I could quietly walk down the sidewalk and cross out of sight of the market. As I entered the alley, I saw another one of the usual dumpsters about twenty feet away. I didn't want to wait that far from the street where the gang member would pass, but I could pull him behind the dumpster out of sight of anyone passing by. That would give me time to do what I needed to do.

****

As it turned out, Marcie owned her storefront and could use it as collateral for a small loan. She now had enough funds to install a video security system that she could monitor from her house and phone. Her phone would let her see what was happening at the restaurant if the alarm went off, so she could call law enforcement. Unfortunately, police response time was slow enough that anyone breaking into her restaurant would probably have already left by the time they arrived. However, if she were there and a break-in occurred, her mother could call 911, even if she couldn't.

The electronics store in her area offered an affordable video surveillance system that suited her needs. That left her enough money for a new handgun. She decided to buy a small, concealable one to carry and a larger, more powerful one to hide in the store. She wasn't going to take any more chances. She also knew that her brother owned an old double-barreled shotgun that had belonged to her father. She hoped he would let her keep it at the house, just in case the gang members decided to target her there.

Heading back to the restaurant with a smile, Marcie felt good about her accomplishments. She hoped she might get a chance to see

Joshua that evening. Since it hadn't been that long since she lost her husband, she felt a little guilty having those kinds of feelings. As much as she had loved him, they had only known each other for less than a year, so the love was not long and deep-seated. There was room in her heart for someone else, but Joshua did not seem like that person, so she didn't know why she was feeling the way she was. She would have to wait and see.

CHAPTER 15

Since the suspected gang member had entered the market, I had seen no one pass or head toward the market that might impede my plans, but now, as I peered around the corner, I could see the market door open and my target struggling out the door with his duffel bag loaded down. The Asian owner was shouting at him in what sounded like his native language as he followed the gang member out the door. Although I couldn't understand what was being said, I guessed that the gang member wasn't paying for the supplies.

The store owner was illuminated by the store's lights as he pulled out his cell phone. The gang member, noticing this and suspecting the owner was calling the police, dropped his duffel bag, reached into his pocket, and pulled out what I suspected was a gun. He grabbed the owner before he could retreat into the store and hit him over the head, causing him to slump to the sidewalk. The gang member then walked over to where the phone had landed and stomped on it several times. Then he went back to his bag, slung it over his shoulder, and headed in my direction.

Knowing my target had a gun didn't worry or frighten me, since when I lunged at the gang member, it would be a complete surprise. I had no doubt I could overpower him. He seemed a bit heavy, possibly due to the clothes he was wearing, and was noticeably shorter than me.

Just as my target reached the edge of the alley where I was hidden, he turned to look back at the market to check if the owner was after him. That put my target back in my control, and it was time to take him down. I slipped up behind him, wrapped one arm around his neck in a chokehold, and grabbed the arm that was holding the gun. I dragged the man back into the alley and behind the dumpster. I forced him to the ground, flipped him onto his face, and held one arm behind his back. As my target started trying to scream, which was difficult because of my chokehold, I pushed his face down into some debris and garbage that had been missed being thrown into the dumpster.

With my target beginning to weaken from his struggles and lack of oxygen, he went limp, resulting in my releasing my grip. I didn't want to kill him. I quickly reached into the man's pocket and pulled out a small Saturday Night Special revolver that could be bought on the black market for a few dollars. They could still be very dangerous, but also quite unreliable.

I took the duffel bag off the man's shoulder and set it aside. Then, following the same method I used with Methhead, I stretched out both of the man's arms, with his hands flat on the concrete. I stomped on both hands, breaking most or all of the bones. I opened the dumpster's lid, and, with some effort since he was heavier than Methhead, I hoisted the man onto my shoulder. I walked a few feet to the dumpster and tossed him inside, then closed the lid. One more gang member was out of commission for the foreseeable future.

I lifted the duffel bag over my shoulder, walked back onto the sidewalk, and headed toward the market. I pulled my Stetson down, shielded my eyes, and pulled my scarf over my mouth so the owner would not identify me. When I arrived at the market door, the owner's wife was helping her husband up off the sidewalk. Blood was running down the side of his head. Then, dropping the duffel bag just inside the market door, I said, "Have a good evening." I crossed the street into the alley where I had been conducting my surveillance and returned to the auto repair store. I needed some rest.

****

Closing time at the restaurant was nearing, and even though Marcie had gone out the back door a few times, there was still no sign of Joshua. She began to wonder if she would ever see him again. That thought weighed heavily on her heart. After checking the alley one last time, she glanced at the calendar on the wall as she headed back into the kitchen. Tomorrow was the court date for the gang members. She was told she didn't need to be there, but she was seriously thinking about going to show them she wasn't scared. She hadn't decided if she was ready for it, and her mother and sister told her to forget it. That wasn't easy for her to do. She just wished Joshua were there to talk to about it.

Arriving home and finally noticing the late hour, Marcie decided to go to bed. Her sister had already left, and her mom was already in bed, so there was no one to talk to about court the next day. Throwing her clothes into a chair in the corner, she slipped into her pajama bottoms and then pulled a long-sleeved, Marine-embossed shirt over her head. She heard a noise at the front door as she headed toward the bathroom. She froze. Were they coming after her again? Grabbing her Glock, which she had taken out of her holster and placed on her nightstand when she first entered her bedroom, she racked the slide to make sure a round was chambered. Moving into the living room, keeping away from the front windows, she peeked out from the edge of the curtain.

Not again, she thought to herself. Relaxing her shoulders, Marcie lowered her weapon and kept it behind her back to keep it out of sight. As she unlocked and opened the front door, she found herself staring up into Officer Duncan's eyes, who had a smile on his face.

"Good evening, Marcie. I hope I'm not calling on you too late?"

"You are. I was just headed for bed, and you probably woke up my mom. I worked late and will answer your question again. No, I will not go out with you!"

Frustrated, he looked up at Marcie and said, "I did not come by to ask you out again. I have gotten the hint. I came to tell you that another gang member has been taken out of commission in the same way as the first one. I just wanted to ask you again if you know who is doing this. This cannot continue."

"No. Once again, I want to assure you that I am not involved in this and do not know who is, but God bless whoever it is. I heard the court would probably do a plea bargain with them, and I don't think that is appropriate justice, but I am not doing anything."

"Okay. I am just doing my job. I know you have a brother who is an Afghanistan veteran. Do you think he could be involved?"

"My brother is in a wheelchair, so no, he couldn't be involved." The disgust in her voice was obvious. "Now, if that is all, I would like to go to bed." She folded her arms across her chest, temporarily forgetting she had a weapon in her hand.

Officer Duncan stepped back a pace from the door. "Okay. I get your point."

"Oh, sorry about that. I did not have this for you. I didn't know who was at the door at first and was afraid it was those gang members coming after me again."

"That's good, you're protecting yourself. I suspect the court date tomorrow will be canceled. I doubt they will show up with two of their gang members out of commission and we have not being able to find the rest of them. I will let you know when a new date has been set."

"Thank you, Officer."

"Thank you, Ma'am."

With that, Marcie closed the door, locked it, and then went back to her bedroom. She suddenly realized she had forgotten to put on her robe in her rush to arm herself. Looking at herself in the mirror, she saw that her long-sleeve nightshirt was a bit threadbare and too revealing. The only good thing was that she hadn't caught Officer Duncan looking at her chest. So maybe there was some saving grace in him after all. Perhaps she should reconsider and go out on a date with him. He had spent a lot of time updating her, and she might have judged him unfairly. She'd have to think about that. But now, it was time for bed.

****

On my way back to the auto repair shop where I had recently taken refuge, I was struck by another severe headache. It felt like someone had hit me in the head with a sledgehammer. Luckily, I was in the alley behind the auto repair shop when I collapsed and lost consciousness. If I had been out on the street, someone might have seen me and taken me to the hospital, and I couldn't let that happen.

I didn't know how long I lay there, but I suspected it was only ten or fifteen minutes. When I woke up, I was extremely tired and cold, barely able to make it the rest of the way down the alley and into the building.

The weather had turned a bit warmer, but because of the chill I caught while unconscious, I kept my heavy jacket on and went to the big chair where I had been sleeping. My head still throbbed, which made me feel a little nauseous, so I wasn't in the mood to eat. I had some aspirin in my coat pocket, so I grabbed it and swallowed two. My last thought before I fell asleep was that I probably needed to stay in bed for a day before chasing after another gang member. It usually took me a day to recover from the headaches.

Each time I had a headache, it seemed to last a little longer than the previous one—or at least the recovery time did. I thought that if this kept happening, one morning I wouldn't wake up at all. I might have welcomed that a few weeks ago, but I wasn't so sure today, especially since Marcie had come into my life. I might be able to make it to Marcie's restaurant for some warmth and a good meal. I'd see how I felt tomorrow night.

The next day, still tired from a restless night's sleep, I got up from my chair, recognizing I needed to fuel this body of mine. I hadn't felt like eating last night, but now I knew I had to replenish my strength with food. It was still early, so maybe I could convince Marcie to give me at least something to get through the day. It would still be better if she weren't there to ask me questions about what I was doing. I would have to take the risk.

Suspecting the restaurant was still closed, I went to the alley door and knocked. I waited a few seconds, and just as I was about to knock again, I heard it being unlocked. Then, it opened slightly.

"Hi, Joshua. How are you?"

I was relieved it wasn't Marcie who answered the door, but her sister instead. "I'm fine. I wondered if I could get something to eat this morning—even though I haven't been able to spend the night keeping an eye on the restaurant."

"I'm sure we can find you something. What have you been doing that has kept you away? Marcie was asking about you."

"Oh, I just had to help out some of my veteran friends. I should be done in a couple more days. Then I can come back at night to resume my guard duties."

"That might not be necessary, Joshua. Marcie has purchased a video security system to have her restaurant under surveillance twenty-four-seven."

"Hmm. Guess Marcie won't need me around anymore," I said with evident dejection.

"Well, don't necessarily think that. I suspect she might still find something for you to do to cover the cost of your meals. Meanwhile, let me go find you something."

With a paper sack of restaurant leftovers, I went straight to the hideout in the Five-and-Dime across the street from the gang headquarters. I wanted to watch them from across the street for a while to see if I noticed any actions on their part that would suggest they had found my access to the foul toilet. It would also give me time to rest before the evening activities.

CHAPTER 16

This was becoming a habit. Marcie was late getting up again, and as she padded into the kitchen, she saw that her mother was already gone, probably to prep breakfast at the restaurant. Her coffee cup sat next to a half-full pot, so she poured herself a cup and took a large gulp to wake herself up with the caffeine jolt.

Most of the swelling on her face had subsided. When she pressed on various spots, she felt only a slight tenderness. It also seemed like she could now take a deep breath without her cracked ribs protesting. As much as she wanted to stay around the house a little longer, she saw on the kitchen clock that it was already 9:00 a.m., and the installation guy was supposed to arrive at 10:00 a.m. to set up her new video surveillance system. She didn't need to be there when he installed it since he would know where to place each camera for the best results. However, he would help her upload the app to monitor the video feed from anywhere. It was time to get moving.

Arriving at her restaurant an hour later, Marcie entered as the last breakfast customers were finishing.

"Morning, sweetheart! How did you sleep last night?"

"It's getting better every night, Mom. I couldn't just lounge around this morning because the installer was supposed to be here any minute. How was breakfast?"

"Not bad! We had about the normal turnout. The customers were glad we were back up and running, and they all asked about you."

"That's nice! I…" Marcie didn't get to finish her sentence as she heard the door open behind her. She quickly turned toward the door with her right hand moving toward her Glock.

"Whoa! Take it easy! I'm the installer. Sorry, I'm late."

Marcie relaxed her body, removing her hand from her weapon. "Sorry for that. I've been a little skittish since the attack. I'm Marcie, and I called to schedule the installation of the video cameras. I will be here if you have any questions, but then I will need help with the monitoring app for my phone."

"Great. I will get started and let you know when I'm ready to activate everything."

Marcie continued into the kitchen, filled a cup with coffee, and plopped down in a chair. "That was a little embarrassing," she said to herself.

While she kept drinking her coffee, Fran stepped out of the bathroom. "Did I hear you talking to yourself a minute ago, sister?"

"Yes. I almost embarrassed myself in front of everyone when I started to draw my weapon on the video installer. I had my back to the door, and he surprised me a little. I'm still a little jittery."

"That's understandable. You encountered worse situations in Iraq and recovered from them, so this will fade away in due time. Oh, by the way, Joshua stopped by this morning. He was looking for something to eat. I gave him a sack of leftover stuff."

This news perked Marcie up. "Did he say where he's been?"

"He said he has been helping out a couple of veteran friends. He indicated that he should be finished in a couple of days and would be able to start spending the night again. I told him about the surveillance equipment and that you probably wouldn't need him anymore."

"Why did you tell him that, Fran? He might never come back!" She knew she shouldn't be angry at her sister.

"No, I told him you might find something else for him to do, so I think he will be back."

Relaxing a little, she responded, "Okay. Thanks. I need to talk to him, though."

"Why is that?" Maxine said as she entered the kitchen, hearing only part of the conversation.

"I learned some things about his time in Afghanistan that I want to ask him about. Once I talk to him, I'll tell you everything. For now, I want to keep it to myself."

"That's great. Keep us in suspense."

"I don't intend for it to be that way, but I want to confirm some things before I tell you all about it."

"I think you have taken a bit of a liking to him, Marcie. Haven't you?"

"Not really. Well, maybe a little bit. He has been so helpful, but I don't think he is my type. Look at how he is living. And he seems to have some serious medical problems. I am too busy to be getting involved with someone like him."

"Okay, if you say so, my loving daughter. Just let us know if we can help in any way."

"Thanks, Mom. I will. Now, let's decide what we'll have for dinner so I can go to the store and buy the necessary supplies."

Marcie spent the rest of the morning making a list of needed groceries, but that didn't keep her from feeling very conflicted about Joshua. She needed to find a way to see and talk to him.

****

I had moved a chair near the front window where I could relax and still see across the street through the hole I had cut in the paper covering the window. This allowed me to relax, eat, and watch the gang activity. Apart from Ponytail coming outside several times, probably looking for his gang member who went to the store last night, the day was uneventful. Ponytail could look all he wanted. He wasn't likely to see his guy for some time. I didn't know if the police or anyone else had found the man in the dumpster yet. I imagined that once he regained consciousness, it would be hard for the guy to climb out of the dumpster with smashed hands.

As shadows began to walk across the buildings and street in front of me, I felt much better than I had in the morning. Once darkness had descended, I prepared to access the room next to the grocery store.

Thirty minutes later, after retaking a roundabout route, I entered the hair and nail salon with as much stealth as possible in case my entry hole had been discovered. Although this area seemed quiet, I picked up an old broom, breaking the head off as a weapon in case someone awaited me on the other side of the brick wall. I recall using a broom as a weapon not too long ago.

Squatting down, I waited and listened for ten minutes, but heard nothing suspicious. Then, crawling through the hole, I made my way to the wall where I had replaced the large sheet of drywall I had previously removed. I put it back in place when I left, hoping to contain the foul odor in the bathroom. It worked. The area where I stood no longer smelled bad, but as I started to climb into the bathroom, the smell hit me again. It smelled like something rotten, almost making me gag.

Now, in the bathroom, I couldn't hear any noise from the gang headquarters. There was no music, no voices, and no signs of anyone moving around. I hadn't seen anyone leave through the front door before returning here, except Ponytail making a brief appearance, but they might have all left for some reason while I was on my way. Maybe they went out to look for their missing gang member. I planned to teach Ponytail a lesson if he was the only one left.

Approaching the bathroom door, I slowly turned the handle, hoping it hadn't rusted and wouldn't squeak when I opened it. My wish was granted. As I cautiously opened the door just a crack, I couldn't see much since the grocery store area was dark. No lamps or candles were lit. I always carried a small penlight flashlight, which I rarely used, but this was one of those times it would come in handy.

With the penlight at its lowest illumination, I opened the door wider and crept into the room. All indications to my senses told me no one was there. Shining the light around the room disclosed that the place was a mess. These gang members were not very good housekeepers. A couple of mattresses were on the floor by one wall, and several cots were lined up against another wall. It looked like a table had been constructed from shelving boards, and some folding chairs were haphazardly arranged around it.

Not knowing how much time I had, I began searching the store. Several pot and meth pipes were sitting out on shelving units and counters. I could smell rotting garbage coming from somewhere, but I couldn't see any. There were only three doors in evidence. One door was unmarked, while the others had the appropriate gender names posted on them. I walked over and carefully opened the unmarked door, only to discover that it was the source of the smell. It was a closet they were using as a dumpster. They seemed too lazy to take out their trash and dispose of it in the dumpster down the alley.

A further search of the main room revealed one bag containing several ounces of marijuana and another with several individual packages of meth. I decided to make them wonder what happened to their drugs when they returned, so I placed both packages in my jacket pockets. Since there was nothing else to see, I went back to the men's bathroom and then through the walls to the hair salon.

As I gained access to the alley, I stopped at the first drain I found and dumped the drugs I had taken from the grocery store into the drain. It would be hard to explain if I got caught with that stuff. Retracing my steps, I returned to my Five-and-Dime hideout without incident and resumed my seat to watch for the gang members to return.

After a brief time, four gang members shuffled down the dark sidewalk to the front door of the grocery store. Although I could not see their faces due to the dim light and heavy overcast, their actions indicated they were unhappy campers.

Lights flashed inside the grocery store, and within minutes, Ponytail burst open the front door, rushing out and scanning the street. His right hand gripped a handgun of some kind. I also heard angry shouting as Ponytail returned to the now-lit grocery. I couldn't make out what was being said, but I didn't need to guess why they were angry. Their drugs were gone. Now, the question was whether they would open the door into the foul men's toilet and find my access, and if so, how I would know. Finally, not getting any answers outside on the sidewalk, Ponytail went back into the grocery, slamming the door behind him.

I now understood how many gang members I was dealing with. I had taken two out, so four wouldn't be too difficult to handle, but I had to assume they were all well-armed. I only had the small Saturday Night Special I had taken from the gang member at the market. I needed to think carefully about my next move. Deciding I had done enough damage for one night and not wanting to risk returning to the fabric shop next to the grocery, I exited the back of the building and went back to my auto repair residence.

As I walked through the dark streets, trying to stay dry under the overhangs of buildings, I thanked God for saving me from another painful headache. They never came at regular intervals but seemed to happen whenever I lost my temper and my anger took over my mind. No matter what I did, I couldn't seem to keep my anger under control. I don't remember having this problem while on active duty. My buddies, some of whom had sacrificed their lives for their country and are no longer here, often called me the 'cool cat,' especially under fire. My anger flare-ups must be linked to my PTSD, even though I take medication for it. I suspect that one day, an attack will hit me so hard that it will be the last thing I experience on earth. Well, it didn't look like that would happen tonight as I accessed the hole in the alley wall behind the repair shop and sank into my large, soft recliner. I prayed for a good night's sleep.

CHAPTER 17

After a good night's sleep, I woke up early, just after 6:00. I realized I hadn't eaten since the previous afternoon. I was starving. Although I hoped not to run into Marcie, I decided to see if I could get something to eat at her restaurant. On the other hand, I missed her. She had become a spark in my otherwise dull and unremarkable life. I didn't want to answer many questions, which she kept asking.

My curiosity about what ultimately happened to the two gang members I had taken out drove me to look for either Rafe or Wolf, whichever I could find. They were around more people and probably had heard some rumors. They might also have heard if any gang members were searching for me. Even though the remaining gang members didn't seem too sharp, Ponytail might have figured out what happened to his two disabled gang members based on their encounter with me in the restaurant that first night. Rafe or Wolf might have caught wind of something.

As much as I needed something to eat and figured that if I got to the restaurant early, I could grab something from Marcie's sister or mother before Marcie went to work, I was closer to where I might find Rafe. The homeless shelter Rafe often stayed at was only five minutes away, but when I arrived, I couldn't find anyone who had seen him. I did see Morgan, another veteran I had helped a few times, so I walked up to him where he was leaning against the outside wall of the shelter, smoking a cigarette.

"Those things are going to kill you, Morg. I keep telling you to kick that habit."

"Yeah, yeah, I know, but I don't have many bad habits or pleasures, and it keeps me going. So, who will notice if I lose a couple of years?"

"I will notice, and so will your other friends. Just give it some thought, okay?"

"Okay, okay. Just don't keep bugging me about it."

"Agreed. Now, I have been looking for Rafe without any success. Have you seen him lately?"

"Saw him yesterday and last night, but not this morning. What's up?"

"He gave me some information on some local gang members who have been terrorizing a friend and her restaurant. I was wondering if he had heard anything about them."

"I don't know if he has, but I sure have. It's the talk of the town. One of the guys saw the police show up a few blocks away the other night and take someone out of a dumpster. The police also interviewed the owners of a nearby grocery store. The guy the police found tried to steal from the store owner with a bunch of food and booze. Someone intervened and stopped the whole incident. The store owner did not see what happened to the thief and couldn't identify the person who helped."

"That's interesting, Morg. Have you heard of any gang members coming around causing other trouble?"

"Yes. Mary over there had a run-in with them last night. Four guys approached her, asking questions about someone. She said that when she didn't have the right answers for them, they roughed her up, knocking one of her teeth out. She will probably talk with you."

"Thanks, Morg. I will do that."

"What are you into, Joshua? Are you causing trouble again? Do you need any help?"

"No, I'm good, but thanks for the offer."

Joshua then asked Morg for a couple of the medications he took for his PTSD, if he could spare them. He reached into his jacket pocket, pulled out a couple of containers, and dropped some pills into Joshua's hand. "I'll replace them when I get a chance. Thanks, Morg." I then walked over to Mary, sitting by the wall, smoking a corn cob pipe, and squatted beside her.

"Morning, Mary. I'm Joshua. Morgan over there told me you had a run-in with some punks asking you a bunch of questions. Can you tell me about it?"

"Yeah, I know who you are," she said with a sly look in her eyes and a crooked smile, which was something I suspected might have led to the beating she got. "I think they were asking about you. But I didn't tell them a damn thing. I got this for my trouble," she said, opening her mouth and showing the gap where a tooth used to be.

"Oh, I am so sorry, Mary, but thank you for keeping quiet. You could have saved yourself a lot of trouble if you had just told them about me."

"Ain't no way I was going to do that. I have heard you always seem to be helping folks on the streets, so keeping quiet was the least I could do."

"Well, thanks again, Mary. Can you describe any of them?"

"Naw. It was pretty dark and raining. One big guy had a ponytail, though. He was the one who knocked my tooth out."

Great. "Thanks, my lady," I said as I patted Mary on the shoulder and leaned down to whisper in her ear. "Soon, you won't have to worry about ever seeing them again." Then, standing back up, I headed down the street toward Marcie's restaurant. I didn't see the crooked grin on Mary's face turn into a broad smile and a chuckle.

****

Finishing her second cup of coffee for the morning, Marcie picked up her phone and opened the app that monitored the new video surveillance cameras at her restaurant. It took her a few minutes to log in, but then, scrolling through the app, she found nothing unusual. No one had disturbed her business last night.

After dropping her phone into her purse, rinsing out her coffee cup, and leaving it in the sink, she turned toward her mom, who was standing at the door and putting on her coat. She emphatically stated, "I'm coming in with you this morning. I am feeling good and need to start helping more."

Seeing Marcie's look and knowing she could not talk her out of it, Maxine smiled and said, "Come on then, or we're going to be late."

As Maxine pulled up in front of the restaurant, a police car arrived behind her. "Oh, oh. What did I do?" she asked.

They stepped out of the car and looked toward the police vehicle when Officer Duncan emerged and walked over to them. "Good morning, ladies. Don't get excited. You didn't do anything. I was just doing a drive-by to check on your business."

As Maxine unlocked the restaurant's front door and entered, Marcie walked over to Duncan. "Well, thank you for that and for looking out for me, Officer Duncan. I guess the least I can do for all your help is to let you treat me to dinner." Seeing the surprised look on his face, she continued. "I know I have turned your invitation down several times, but I probably misjudged you. It must be after our dinner rush when Mom and Fran can clean up. Will tomorrow night be all right?"

Slightly flustered and surprised, Officer Duncan had trouble uttering a word but finally managed, "Yes. Yes! That would be fine. My shift is off early, so give me a time."

"Make it 19:00, then."

"I will be here. See you then."

Marcie noticed that as Officer Duncan turned to return to his patrol car, he seemed to have a little skip in his step. She smiled as she turned and entered the restaurant behind her mom.

****

I had just knocked on the alley door of Marcie's restaurant without getting a response. Then, hearing voices, I edged over to the corner of the alley and peered around the brick wall. I could see a police car parked on the curb with an officer standing very close to Marcie, talking. I couldn't hear much, but I did hear Marcie say something to the effect of, 'See you tomorrow night.'

That looked very friendly, I thought to myself. *She must be dating this police officer.* As the officer turned to return to his patrol car, I pulled my head back behind the brick wall. I couldn't afford to be seen. After moving back down the alley, I squatted behind the dumpster. It's not like I ever thought I could have a real relationship with Marcie, but continuing any relationship with her, even as a friend, puts me in danger of getting caught. I couldn't let that happen.

Remaining on my heels, leaning against the brick wall by the dumpster, I wondered whether to get something to eat from Marcie or look for food elsewhere. Before I could decide, the alley door of the restaurant creaked open, and Marcie stepped out.

"Joshua," she said as she walked over to me. "Are you alright?"

Pulling myself to my feet, I responded, "I'm fine. How are you?"

"I'm good. I have almost completely recovered and am back working at the restaurant. Why don't you come in and get something to eat?"

"You are probably busy. I don't want to bother you," I said and turned to leave.

"No, no. I'm not. Please come in, and I'll get you some breakfast."

Pausing, I turned, saying, "Is that police officer still here? He can't see me."

"No. He left. It is safe, and you can stay in the kitchen."

Deciding that my hunger was overcoming my fear of the police, I accepted her offer of breakfast. "Okay. I guess I can."

Reaching out, she took my hand, led me to the restaurant door, and into the kitchen. Guiding me to a chair, she said, "Just sit. I will bring you some coffee and then fix you something." When she looked at the coffee pot, she saw it was still percolating. Turning back to me, she said, "It will be a couple of minutes for the coffee."

"That's fine." I hung my Stetson on a nearby chair and shrugged out of my jacket.

Marcie tossed some eggs into a skillet and placed slices of bacon on a grill that Fran had already turned on. Then, she grabbed some ingredients for an omelet from the fridge. As the bacon sizzled and the eggs popped in the butter, Marcie poured a mug of coffee and set it in front of me.

"I wanted to talk to you about something, Joshua. You may be upset with me, but I checked with a couple of friends of mine who are still in the Marine Corps. They told me some things about you. Some exciting things, and I just wanted to confirm them."

I had the mug of coffee to my lips as Marcie talked, but I immediately pulled it away and set it down hard on the table, spilling some of the coffee onto it. "What! What have you done?"

"I'm sorry. I have just grown fond of you, and with all your help, I've become eager to learn more about you. I didn't mean to offend you." Marcie had put her hands up in front of her mouth, and I could see tears in her eyes.

Calming my nerves, I said, "I'm sorry, but you had no right to do that. My life is private. Besides, you're seeing a police officer, so there's nothing between us." I stood, grabbed my Stetson off the chair, and headed for the alley door.

Marcie rapidly rose from her chair, reaching out to me. "No… I'm not… no, we aren't…" but before she could get her point across, I was out the door, slamming it behind me.

****

"What was that all about, Marcie?" Maxine asked as she hurried up to her.

Marcie sank back into her chair with her head in her hands. Then, tearfully, she lifted her head. "I crossed a line with him, Mom. I looked into Joshua and found some interesting details about him, and I wanted to talk to him about them, but he got upset and stormed out. What have I done?"

Maxine put her arms around Marcie and held her while she sobbed. Finally, drying her eyes, Marcie stood up and asked her mom and sister to sit down. Collecting herself, she told them what she had discovered about Joshua, his medals, and her suspicions that he may have been the Marine who had saved her brother.

A lengthy discussion about this information went on until Fran reminded everyone to start breakfast. After wiping her face and tying on an apron, Marcie began preparing for the breakfast crowd. Deep inside, she regretted what she had done. She had hurt Joshua and violated his privacy so deeply that she wondered if he could ever forgive her. She was afraid she might never find out the answer to that.

CHAPTER 18

I stumbled down the alley with my head pounding and my body shaking all over. It wasn't just from anger but also from frustration for lashing out at Marcie. I expected that crippling headache to hit me any second, but the serious kind stayed in the background this time. I was angrier at myself than I was at Marcie. Maybe someday I could go back to her and apologize. But for now, I still have a mission to finish. I no longer felt the hunger that had troubled me earlier that morning; my mission came first.

On my way back to the auto repair shop, I found enough to eat in another dumpster behind a bakery to satisfy my growling stomach. I had decided to get some more sleep and wait until dark to pursue the remaining gang members. If I succeeded, I could try to reconcile with Marcie. If not, that would likely be the end of my efforts to help others and improve their quality of life.

When I finally woke up, my old military-style watch read 1900 hours. I grabbed a water bottle to hydrate and thought about my next move. I wasn't sure I wanted to confront all four gang members at once, but I'd have the element of surprise if I caught them sleeping. Finally, pulling myself out of the recliner, I searched the shop for a weapon. I didn't want to use the handgun because it might be unreliable. I'd be safer without it. Some tools were lying around, but nothing seemed suitable for my purpose.

Just as I was about to give up and check the alleys for something to use as a weapon, I found a tractor tire iron, which was about three feet long, that had fallen between a storage rack and the wall. It was the right length and would withstand any punishment I might give it, especially against a soft target.

Tossing the tire iron from hand to hand, I felt its weight and got a sense of it. I could use it to jab, hit, or throw if needed. I could also defend against a knife attack, but a firearm would be a problem. It wouldn't offer much protection against bullets. Well, it was the best I could find.

Sitting back down in my chair, I closed my eyes, brought my hands together, and asked God to guide me on my mission, to protect me, and to give me the strength I needed to succeed, even though I wasn't sure what success would look like at this point. Opening my eyes, I reached down to pick up the iron bar from the floor where I had placed it and headed out through the metal siding into the alley. I didn't take much care in reassembling the metal to hide my entrance, figuring that if I succeeded, I wouldn't be returning to this place, and if I failed, I certainly wouldn't need it.

Bypassing the Five-and-Dime store from where I had been watching the gang headquarters, I cautiously approached the hair and nail salon. I didn't want to walk into an ambush. The shop was empty, and there were no signs suggesting that anyone had been there except me. Before I left last time, I had strung some small pieces of yarn across all the openings that would be hard to see in the dark, and I found they were still in place. That still didn't mean I was safe. Crawling through the wall into the fabric shop, I paused and squatted down to listen. At this point, I could hear no sounds other than the occasional truck passing on the street.

The sheetrock I had put back on the wall that led into the grocery store bathroom was still in place, so after I approached it, I pressed my ear to the wall. There were still no sounds or voices. Carefully setting the iron bar on the floor, I lifted the sheetrock out of its position and moved it to the adjacent wall. The smell hit me hard again, like a slap to the face. I should have prepared for it, but it nearly made me gag. *No time to get squeamish*, I thought to myself.

Retrieving the iron bar, I eased into the bathroom. Then, leaning up against the door, I continued to listen for any activity in the grocery store. I could now hear what sounded like a television. I wondered how they got electricity here, but they probably pirated it from another building. The sound was low, and I could not hear any other voices.

Holding the doorknob in my left hand, I carefully and slowly turned it until the door was free from the frame, revealing a narrow gap through which I could see into the room. As luck would have it, the television was across the room facing me, with a couple of chairs and a couch positioned toward the TV, and the occupants facing away from me. I could only see two bodies sitting in chairs and one head on the sofa. Where was the fourth person?

After waiting five minutes with no sign of the fourth man, I decided to take my chance. Pushing the door open, I covered about twenty feet quickly to the chairs and couch. I couldn't tell from the back who was who, so I just started swinging the iron bar, hitting one gang member across the shoulder and neck, knocking him out of his chair and into another gang member who was also seated. They both toppled to the floor. When I pivoted toward the couch, the television light illuminated Ponytail's face, and surprise and fear appeared on his face at the same time.

Ponytail moved faster than I could have ever imagined as his hand shot up from the couch, clutching a handgun, which immediately spat fire and smoke. The sound in the small room was deafening, but I was used to that. What I hadn't felt in a long time was the burning pain in my stomach and along the side of my head as two rounds hit, or at least partly hit, their mark. It didn't stop me as I brought the iron bar crashing down on Ponytail's arm, breaking it and sending the weapon flying.

Ponytail screamed and grabbed his arm as he rolled off the couch, trying to escape. Holding one hand to my chest with blood running down the side of my head, I stumbled after Ponytail, hitting him across the back of his head and grazing his shoulder with the iron bar. I had no intention of killing anyone, even though I was trained to do so. These guys just needed a firm, powerful lesson.

Hearing a noise behind me, I turned just in time to see the gang member who had been sitting in the chair I didn't hit coming at me with a knife. While I was attending to Ponytail, this gang member managed to untangle himself from the chairs and was now almost on top of me. My heavy coat and layers of clothing saved me. The gang member's thrust with the knife punctured through several layers of my clothing but barely scratched my skin. I was able to react with the steel bar, hitting the gang member at the knee and causing him to crash to the floor.

I pulled the knife out of my jacket, where it had been lodged. The gang member was now writhing on the floor, screaming and clutching his shattered knee. Catching my breath, I stood up but still clutched my stomach. Sliding my hand beneath my clothing layers, I felt the wetness of the blood I was losing. If I wanted to survive, I knew I needed to get help.

Quickly surveying the scene, I still hadn't seen the fourth gang member, so maybe he was out on an errand. When he returns and sees this, he might count his lucky stars, turn around, and leave for good. I hoped so and prayed I wouldn't run into him when I left. I wasn't in any shape to fight off another gang member. I knew I had taken down all three and probably all four of the gang members who had terrorized Marcie. Now, I just needed to take care of myself.

Not wanting to risk running into the fourth gang member, I backed through the bathroom, into the fabric store, then through the hair and nail salon, finally entering the alley. Unfortunately, I probably left a trail of blood that could be traced back to me. It was a bit late to worry about that now. I needed to stop the bleeding and find help. As I passed through the fabric shop, I tore off a piece of material from a bolt of cloth, folded it into a small square, and pressed it tightly against my stomach. With my other hand, I reached behind my back to check if the bullet was a through-and-through, but felt no pain, blood, or exit wound. As long as I could still think clearly, I headed for Marcie's restaurant. The fluorescent dial on my watch reflected that it was just past 22:00 hours. I prayed I hadn't missed her. If I did, seeing God might not be too far in my future, that is, if He still wanted me.

Arriving in the alley behind the restaurant, I could feel myself growing weaker. My hand reached for the piece of material I had used as a makeshift compression bandage, soaked with blood. I might have slowed the bleeding, but I hadn't stopped it. Now, leaning against the alley door, I knocked again. There was no answer. I knocked once more, a little harder, yet still no response as I slid into a sitting position on the concrete. My strength was fading as I knocked one last time, using what little energy I had left.

****

"Are you and Mom just about finished back there?" Marcie hollered at her sister, who was sitting in the dining area, finishing a cup of coffee. It had been a busy day, and she was tired. She needed to get home and get some rest. She now realized she hadn't fully recovered from her attack, and she wasn't giving her body the proper time to heal. She guessed she should have listened to her doctor.

"We're finished," Fran responded. "Let me double-lock the back door and get our coats."

Marcie had thought about Joshua several times during the day, but she didn't know how to correct her early outbursts at him. She could try to find him during the day, but had no idea where he hung out. Deciding she would try the homeless shelters to see if she could find someone who knew him, she took her coffee cup to the kitchen to wash it out. Her mom and sister were already heading through the dining area when Marcie grabbed her jacket. Seeing them looking at her, she hollered, "I'm coming."

Just as Marcie reached the front door behind her sister and mom, she stopped. "What was that?"

"What was what, Marcie?" her mom asked.

"I heard a noise. Banging or pounding." Standing half in the restaurant and half out on the sidewalk, she decided she was hearing things and continued onto the sidewalk. "Wait. There it is again."

Rushing back into the restaurant with her mom and sister hot on her heels, Marcie approached the alley door. She paused and listened, then heard a faint tapping outside. Flinging the locks open, Marcie drew her weapon and flung the door wide.

Joshua, leaning against the door semi-conscious, fell through the open door into the kitchen. Marcie holstered her weapon after looking up and down the alley for any threats, then knelt, taking Joshua's bloody head in her hands. "Joshua! What happened?"

"Need your help, Marcie," Joshua managed to say through a dry mouth and lips covered partly with blood from the near-miss head wound. Joshua's jacket fell open, and Marcie could now see the blood-soaked cloth on his stomach.

"Mom, call 911! Quick! Fran, get me a towel from the kitchen and the first-aid kit!"

With a thicker compression bandage on the stomach wound and a wet cloth to wipe the blood off his face, Marcie sat on the kitchen floor with Joshua's head in her lap, talking to him and trying to find out what happened, but by then, he had become completely unconscious. Marcie could now hear sirens in the distance. She prayed they wouldn't arrive too late.

CHAPTER 19

Pacing back and forth in the waiting room, Marcie wiped tears from her eyes as her mom and sister stood and walked over to her, pulling her into their arms. The doctor had just updated them about Joshua's condition; he was critical. The head wound was minor, but the stomach wound was high up in the stomach, and the bullet had hit a rib, fracturing it. The bullet fragment broke apart, and one piece angled toward his heart. The doctor informed them that Joshua was undergoing very delicate surgery at that moment. It was uncertain whether the bullet fragment near his heart could be safely removed without causing more damage.

Hearing the squeak of a wheelchair, Marcie turned around to see her brother rolling down the hallway toward them. He had been fitted with his new prosthetic leg but wasn't yet skilled enough to walk well, so he still depended on his wheelchair. Rolling up to Marcie, he locked his chair as Marcie knelt by him and he embraced her.

"How's he doing, kid? Is he going to make it?"

Wiping one more tear from her cheek, she replied, "We don't know. He's in surgery now, and it's going to be tough. A bullet fragment is lodged near his heart, and doctors are afraid that if they try to remove it, they might cause him more harm. It's just a waiting game now."

Unlocking his chair, John rolled to the row of chairs against the wall, pulling Marcie with him. "Sit!" he ordered her. "We just have to pray that the good Lord will see fit to allow him to stay with us a little longer."

"I feel so bad, John. The last thing we discussed was that I asked him some questions about Afghanistan, and he became distraught and stormed out of the restaurant. I didn't realize how strong my feelings had become for him until this happened."

"Really?" John questioned. "How did this come about?"

"It has been everything he has done for me. Over time, he seemed to be a kindred spirit. Now I will tell you, Mom, and Fran, something I've been concealing until I could confirm it."

"You have been withholding something from us?" Fran asked.

"Yes, until I was sure, and I still am not. I found out that Joshua was responsible for saving several of his Marine unit members' lives in Afghanistan when an IED blew up their Humvee. Because of the timeline, I think it might have been the incident where you lost your leg, John."

Aside from the other ambient sounds typical to any hospital corridor, there was silence around Marcie and her brother.

Finally, John said, "You are kidding me. How could that be? You said his name was Joshua. I don't recall anyone in our unit with that name. Now that I think about it, we had one guy who fit his physical description, but I never made the connection until now. Everyone called him Cowboy because he always wore this dirty, beat-up Stetson whenever we weren't out on a mission or patrol."

"Yes! Yes! That's right!" Marcie shouted, then realized she was in the hospital and quieted down. "Joshua is always wearing this old Stetson that has seen better days. I also learned he was awarded the

Congressional Medal of Honor for his actions that day. Even though he was seriously wounded, he saved all eight of his Marines in that Humvee, as well as preventing the Taliban from overrunning another unit that was trying to save you guys."

"Wow! Won't that be something if you are right!"

With the adrenaline rush subsiding, all four sat pondering the latest revelation. Then John spoke. "Have you asked Joshua about all this, Marcie?"

"I tried last night, but he got upset and took off. I don't understand how he ended up homeless out on the street."

"Sometimes, even if the physical wounds aren't too serious, mentally, some soldiers have trouble surviving when they return to the States."

"I have to agree. Once, at the restaurant, he collapsed with a severe headache and was unconscious on the floor for at least ten minutes. He wouldn't talk about it beyond saying it had happened before. He also seemed to have anger management issues. Supposedly, he had medication for it, but it didn't always work."

"As I recall, the man I'm thinking about, who was in our Humvee when it blew up, was married but didn't have any children. He always talked about her and looked forward to returning to the States to be with her. I think that was going to be his last deployment. It was either his second or third trip to the Sandbox. I wonder what happened to his wife."

"I don't recall him wearing a ring."

"Oh, so you looked for that," her mother stated.

"Well, yes. At some point, I did take note of that, but it wasn't until after he had been staying at the restaurant to watch it at night."

"Do you have a picture of him?"

"No, I never did get one. Once we see him, hopefully, you can tell if he is the same Marine who saved you."

"I'm not sure I will be able to. I was unconscious after the IED exploded and didn't know who was helping me, but if it were Cowboy, I would recognize him."

"Based on what some of my Marine buddies still on active duty told me, he helped everyone in the Humvee, so he probably helped you, too."

"Wow. This is so weird. I owe him my life, then!"

"As do I. His help the night I was attacked likely saved my life also."

Two hours later, Marcie, her mom, brother, and sister were startled, a little out of their thoughts and prayers, by a doctor who approached and stood before them.

"Are you the family of the man I just operated on?"

"Ah… yes," Marcie finally managed to respond. She knew it was the only way the doctor would give them any information about Joshua.

"I just finished the first surgery on him and was able to remove all of the bullet fragments. Soon, we will move him to the ICU. We need to monitor him closely for the next twenty-four to forty-eight hours, but he can make it through this."

Marcie's mother had picked up on the doctor's comment about the first surgery. "What do you mean, the first surgery, doctor?"

"Due to the minor head wound, we decided to do an MRI of his head to ensure there were no other internal brain injuries or damage. We were able to spot a tiny piece of metal, probably from an old wound, that currently rests against his amygdala. That part of the brain helps coordinate responses to things in your environment, especially those that trigger an emotional response. That part of the brain also plays a key role in fear and anger.

"That may account for it," Marcie stated somewhat dumbfoundedly.

"Account for what?"

"He was seriously injured in Afghanistan by an IED. Once he returned to the U.S. and recovered from his injuries, he ended up homeless and sometimes seemed to have anger issues and severe headaches. He collapsed once in front of me and was unconscious for at least ten minutes. He told me the VA doctors didn't know what the problem was, other than it was just part of the PTSD he suffered."

"That might explain it. It's such a tiny fragment that it could easily be missed. Once he recovers from the gunshot wound, we will consider going in to attempt the removal of this small piece. It will be very risky, with a high chance of failure. We'll leave it up to him whether he wants us to try. Now, I need to get back to work. It will be an hour before anyone can see him, so you might want to get something to eat and then come back."

"I'm going to wait here. You guys can all get something to eat. I'm not hungry. Just bring me some coffee when you return."

"Are you sure, honey?"

"I'm sure, Mom. I want to stay."

As John, Maxine, and Fran headed down the hall toward the elevator, the doors opened, and two rather unkempt people exited into the hallway. One was in a wheelchair, and the other was using crutches.

"Excuse us," the man in the wheelchair said as he rolled himself out of the way of the elevator doors. As he did, he noticed John in his wheelchair, rolling up behind his mom and sister.

"Hey, brother. How ya doin'?"

"I'm good." John took a second look at the two men. "You two wouldn't be up here to see Joshua, would you?"

"We are. We heard he was shot and wanted to check on him. We're vets who sometimes come into contact with him on the street. He's always been willing to help us, and we wanted to go and pray for him. Who might you be?"

"I'm John, and this is my mother, Maxine, and my sister, Fran. Sitting over there against the wall is Marcie. Joshua has helped us at Marcie's restaurant several times, and we believe he helped defend her against some thugs who attacked her one night."

"Ohhh, okay. Now I know who you are. Joshua has talked a lot about you and often provides us with food items he gets at your restaurant." Thinking through what he had just said, the man said, "Oops, maybe I shouldn't have said that. Maybe he wasn't supposed to be taking that food."

"No. That's all right. Marcie is dedicated to helping as many people as possible. She opened that restaurant in that location against our best wishes. She needs to feel she is helping others in need."

"She sure has been doing that, according to Joshua. My name is Rafe, by the way, and this is Wolf."

"It's a pleasure to meet you both," John stated. "I am a vet also. I got wounded in Afghanistan, and my sister just learned Joshua may have been in my same unit and saved my life. That is why we are so anxious for his recovery."

Wolf, who had been quiet, responded, "Joshua has had a rough time. He got kicked out of every homeless shelter around because of his anger issues, so we know any help you gave him is greatly appreciated."

"Thanks. We also learned something else from the doctor. He said that one of the bullets had grazed Joshua's head, so they did an MRI to check for other injuries and found a tiny piece of metal in his brain that might have been affecting his anger management. I don't remember exactly where they said it was, but when he recovers from the gunshot wound, they will offer to remove it."

"Well, I hate to say this," Rafe said, "but often God helps good come out of bad. If he hadn't been shot tonight, they might have never found that piece of what is probably shrapnel in his brain. Wow!"

"We will let you all go now. Do you think it will be okay if I talk with Marcie?"

"Of course," Fran responded.

As Rafe and Wolf moved toward Marcie, Maxine, Fran, and John approached the elevator. Just then, the other elevator door opened, and two police officers stepped out, nearly bumping into them.

"Sorry, folks. We weren't watching where we were going."

Fran noticed the name tag on one of the officers' uniforms. "You're Officer Duncan, aren't you?"

"Yes, ma'am, I am. And you are?"

"I'm Fran, Marcie's sister. She is sitting over there. What are you up here for?"

Officer Duncan explained that they were looking into the shooting that resulted in several gang members being seriously injured and one man being shot. They were there to interview the gunshot victim.

"That is Joshua. He is the man who helped Marcie when those gang members broke into her restaurant and attacked her."

Officer Duncan was quiet for a moment, then turned toward his partner. "I knew she couldn't have taken on all four of those guys like she said she did. She was covering for this guy."

Fran looked at her mom and brother and said, "We don't know anything about that. You will have to talk to Marcie." The three of them moved into the elevator, and the doors shut behind them. Fran immediately pulled out her phone and started texting.

"What are you doing, sis?"

"Hush, wait until I have finished." It took a full minute of texting as the elevator descended to the main hospital floor before Fran responded to her brother. As they left the elevator and headed toward the dining room, Fran said, "I was just letting Marcie know what was happening and that Officer Duncan knew about Joshua helping her. That's the least I could do after spilling the beans to him. I hope that doesn't get them in any trouble."

"If what Officer Duncan said is correct about some gang members being seriously injured, Joshua may already be in a heap of trouble. Leave it up to Marcie to get him out of it."

CHAPTER 20

As Officer Duncan approached Marcie, who was sitting in a chair along the wall outside the ward, he noticed she was texting on her phone. He walked up to her, waiting for her to finish what she was doing. When she closed her phone and looked up at him, he asked, "What's the word on this guy? Is he going to pull through?"

Not wanting to give anything away, Marcie replied, "I don't know. He's still in surgery and is listed in critical condition."

"You know, your actions have interfered with the conduct of an investigation by the police department. That could get you thrown in jail."

Marcie could tell that Officer Duncan was not being too serious, as he had a grin. "Why, Officer, I have no idea what you're talking about."

"To begin with, you didn't handle all four of those gang members by yourself that first night, as you told me that you did. This Joshua helped you out. Since he was a witness, we would have had a better chance of getting some action against them in court."

"Officer, since he did me a big favor by helping with those thugs, I owed him one in return. He was very clear that he wanted no contact with law enforcement, so to respect that, I kept his name out of it." She held out her hands and said, "So, if I am now a criminal, then slap the cuffs on me right here and take me to jail."

"No, I won't do that, and you know it. But were you also withholding information about those other gang members being attacked by this vigilante?"

"I was not. I suspected he might have been involved, but I haven't seen or spoken to him for several days and don't know what he's been doing. However, with this recent shooting incident, I suspect he was taking them out of commission after they attacked me as a way of protecting me, since the courts didn't seem to be doing a good job of that."

"I tell you what. Let's call a truce. I'm not going to arrest you, and I won't take any action against Joshua until I have talked with him and gotten his side of the story."

"Fair enough," Marcie responded.

"Do you know how he got shot?" Duncan now asked.

"No, he was not very coherent when he came to the alley door of my restaurant. I was more concerned about stopping the bleeding and getting him medical help."

"If you don't mind the company, I will sit with you until someone comes out to update us on his condition. I need to talk to him as soon as he is able."

"I suspect that it could be quite some time since he is still in surgery, and the last time the doctor came out, he didn't seem optimistic about his chances. Even if he survives the surgery, it could be some time before he is awake. If you'd like, I can take your number and call you as soon as possible. That way, you can go about your other duties. I promise I will call you when he wakes up… if he does."

Marcie's last comment caused sadness to flicker across her face, which Duncan clearly noticed. "You seem to have some feelings for this man. At least based on your facial expressions, that would be my guess."

Sitting quietly with her hands clasped in her lap, she finally responded, "I guess I do. He seems like a very nice man who always tries to help others, and I would hate to see him punished for that." After another brief moment of silence, she continued, "I've also found out that he might have been the Marine who saved my brother's life in Afghanistan. I did learn he was awarded the Congressional Medal of Honor for his actions, so that should count for something."

"The Medal of Honor. Are you sure, Marcie? Why in heaven's name is he out on the streets then?"

"I don't have an answer for that. I got the feeling he has some anger issues, and he suffers from severe, debilitating headaches at times. One occurrence was at the restaurant when he went unconscious for several minutes. That, coupled with probable PTSD, probably has prevented him from functioning well in today's society. Oh, and the doctor told me they did an MRI since he had a minor head wound, and they found a tiny piece of metal in his brain, which may have been causing the headaches and blackouts. He said it appeared to be from an old injury."

As Marcie and Officer Duncan continued their discussion, Marcie managed to relax a bit and regain control of her emotions about Joshua. She didn't have a claim on him, but she didn't want him to get a raw deal for what he had been doing to help her.

A half-hour later, with no new updates on Joshua's condition, Officer Duncan finally decided to return to duty and rely on Marcie to call him when Joshua awoke. After Duncan left, Marcie sat, her eyes closed, praying for Joshua. Something about him drew her in, and she prayed he would survive this surgery so she could satisfy these feelings.

"Pardon me, ma'am."

Marcie opened her eyes and looked up at a man in a nice suit and tie, standing over her. "Oh, I'm sorry I didn't see you there," she mumbled.

"That's okay. I'm sorry to bother you, but I was told there's a man in surgery I've been looking for the past couple of weeks. His name is Griggs. Do you know if he's inside, undergoing surgery right now?"

"Let me first ask: Who are you, and why have you been looking for this Griggs guy?"

Sitting down next to her, where Officer Duncan had previously been, he pulled a wallet from his jacket pocket, opened it, and then took out a business card to give to her.

As Marcie looked at the card, she looked back at the man. "Marcus Waller with the Veterans Administration. So, why are you looking for Griggs?"

"Well, I'm a little embarrassed to admit this, but the VA has done a terrible disservice to Griggs. During his treatments and counseling after he returned from Afghanistan, we missed something important. A new doctor we hired was reviewing the files of VA patients who appeared to be having trouble adjusting to society. He was searching for anything that other doctors might have overlooked. He found something in Griggs's file."

"It wouldn't be the failure to spot a small piece of shrapnel in his head that he received in Afghanistan, would it?"

Waller sat still with a stunned look on his face. "Yes, as a matter of fact, it is. How do you know about that?"

"Joshua was shot twice tonight, and since one bullet scraped his skull but didn't penetrate, the surgeons decided to run an MRI just to ensure there were no hidden injuries. They found a tiny piece of metal next to his… I don't recall the name of the brain part, but it's a region that influences anger, temper, and other emotions."

"Well then. Looks like my job has been done for me. Please keep my card and give it to Mr. Griggs when he wakes up. I would still like to talk to him and apologize on behalf of the VA. Do you know what they will do about that piece of metal?"

"The doctor told me that if and when he recovers from the surgery for the other bullet that hit him in the stomach, they will ask him if he wants them to attempt removal of that piece of metal in his brain. The doctor said it is a delicate surgery and could have some negative side effects. They will leave it up to Joshua."

"Very good. Thanks for your help. Please give him my card and tell him I look forward to meeting with him."

"I will, and thank you," Marcie said as Waller rose, shook her hand, and then headed down the hallway toward the elevators.

Marcie leaned her head back against the wall and closed her eyes. She felt tired. Maybe she should go home and rest, but she wanted to stay until Joshua came out of surgery. That was the last thought she had before she drifted off.

Feeling a tap on her shoulder, Marcie's eyes suddenly widened, and she sat up straighter in her chair. The nurse standing in front of her was dressed in surgical scrubs. "Is he alright? Is he okay? Did something happen?"

"Yes, ma'am. Joshua is stable in the ICU and seems to be doing well. He is starting to wake up from the anesthesia. I was told you were waiting to see him at the first available opportunity. There is a waiting area on the third floor outside the ICU where you can wait."

Noticing her name tag, Marcie said, "Thank you, Nurse Bond." She then grabbed her jacket and headed for the elevator. She decided not to call anyone, especially Officer Duncan, until she could talk with Joshua.

****

The squeaky wheel of some cart and the soft clanking of metal on metal brought me out of my deep sleep, or at least that was my first impression. As I pried my eyes open, I did not initially recognize my surroundings. Slowly, my mind cleared, and I knew I was in a hospital. The last thing I remembered was being shot and then struggling on my way to Marcie's restaurant. I remembered nothing after that.

As I tried to sit up in bed, a sharp pain shot through my stomach area. Lying back down, then pulling up my hospital gown, I could see the bandage on my stomach. I instinctively knew the police would show up soon if they weren't already waiting in the hall. I was going to be in big trouble. I needed to get out of here.

Looking around the room, I couldn't see my street clothes. That would make my escape much harder, but maybe my clothes were in the bathroom. Slowly swinging my legs over the side of the hospital bed, I realized I was connected to several tubes, which I would need to disconnect before reaching the bathroom. My first move was to remove the nasal cannula from my nose and set it aside. Then, I pulled the needle connected to the saline bag on a stand out of my arm. That was enough to let me walk to the bathroom. Unfortunately, the sedative hadn't worn off completely. I was hit with dizziness and a headache, causing me to lose my balance and fall to the floor.

I had no idea how long I was on the floor, but when I opened my eyes again, a nurse and a doctor were hovering over me. "And just where do you think you were going, young man?" the doctor asked. "You just got out of surgery an hour ago and need to stay in bed."

"No, I need to get out of here. I can't stay, and I can't pay."

"Depending on your condition, you're not going anywhere for at least forty-eight hours. If you don't agree to stay in bed, I will have the officer who has been up to see you cuff you to the bed frame. So, are you going to stay here?"

Hearing that the police had already been there and were probably waiting outside deflated me as I realized my freedom had finally come to an end. I could also physically feel that I was not up to going anywhere.

After returning me to my bed, as the doctor turned to leave, the nurse said, "There is a young lady who has been outside waiting to see you since you arrived. Can I tell her she's welcome to come in? It can only be for a few moments. You need your rest."

Lying back on my pillows, relegating myself to the reality that I was stuck here, I responded, "Yes. You can let her in."

****

When the nurse told her that Joshua was awake, Marcie quickly stood up from her chair and followed the nurse into the ICU room, where she saw Joshua lying in bed with tubes attached to him. He turned his eyes toward her as she approached the bed. "You are a sight for sore eyes. Sorry, I crashed into your back door last night. I have lost track of time."

Taking Joshua's hand, she said, "I am so glad you felt you could come to me. I have been worried sick about you. How are you doing?"

"I think I will live. I was unsure I wanted to, but seeing you here changed my mind."

"You'd better, you big oaf. Especially after I waited all night for you to get out of the surgery and wake up. Speaking of that, I have to call Officer Duncan. He came by and wants to talk with you. What have you done?"

****

Realizing it would all come out anyway, I decided to be honest with Marcie. "Over the last couple of weeks, I have been meting out some punishment for those gang members who attacked you. I suspected not much was going to happen to them in court, and I could not stand to let them get away with what they did to you."

"So, you were involved in the damage to those first two gang members who were beaten up. Officer Duncan asked me if I knew who was involved, and although I suspected it was you, I lied to him."

"Yes, it was me, but in each case, I stopped them while committing a crime. They were both robbing store owners, and I stopped them. The first one, I called Methhead, was also molesting the store owner's daughter. The last group had drugs and guns in their little headquarters. I took several of them on at once, and they got the better of me. Well, not exactly. I put them all out of commission for quite a while. I don't think I killed anyone. I guess I could be called a vigilante."

"As much as all that gives me a little peace of mind knowing they aren't going to bother me again, I wish you hadn't done that since you are now in a lot of hot water."

"I've been there before. I will have to take my medicine."

"Well, I've spoken enough. I'll leave you to rest, but only if you promise to stay in bed and not try to leave. Otherwise, I'll be camped right outside your room."

"I will stay," I agreed.

"I also will wait at least an hour before calling Officer Duncan so you can rest."

****

With that, Marcie quickly kissed my hand and then left the room. She needed food, sleep, and to update her family about Joshua. Her heart was pounding as if she had just run a marathon. She felt so little control over her emotions for Joshua; maybe she shouldn't try to control them and just let them carry her wherever they will. If she did that, what if his feelings didn't match hers? Plus, he could end up in jail. She could lose another man in her life. That was not something she felt she could handle right now.

165

CHAPTER 21

Once Marcie left, I reflected on what had just happened. The love and compassion I saw in Marcie's face, along with her emotional behavior, sent my emotions tumbling like a rockslide. I am not currently in a position to get involved with anyone.

After the nurse who had just taken my vitals left the room, I rested on my pillows and drifted off to sleep. I didn't know how long I had slept, but it was dark when I dozed off, and now the sun shone brightly through my hospital window. Reaching for the glass next to my bed, I drank the much-needed water through the straw. As I was putting the glass back on the table, there was a knock on the door.

"Good morning, Mr. Griggs. Are you up to having a visitor?" Officer Duncan walked into the room without waiting for me to answer.

"I guess I am, since you are already in my room. What can I do for you?" When I adjusted my body to move the pillows higher up behind my head, I expelled a groan resulting from the pain that stabbed through my stomach. "Oh, that didn't feel good."

"Here, let me help you," Duncan said as he walked over and adjusted the pillows so I sat more upright in the hospital bed.

"I just have a few questions for you, but unfortunately, I have to advise you of your rights," Duncan said. "You have the right to remain silent and are not required to answer any questions. You also have the right to an attorney and to have an attorney present during questioning. If you cannot afford an attorney, one will be appointed for you.

"Do you understand your rights as I have read them to you?"

"Yes, I do."

"Do you wish to have an attorney present?"

"I can't afford one, so you can ask me questions without one. I can stop and request an attorney any time, correct?"

"Absolutely."

"First off, I need to ask you about two gang members that were…"

"Excuse me," a voice interrupted from the open doorway behind Officer Duncan. "Joshua, you do have an attorney, and he is present. Officer, please wait until I have a chance to counsel my client before you ask any more questions. And would you mind stepping outside and closing the door behind you so we can have some privacy?"

Officer Duncan looked surprised and frustrated but responded, "Be glad to. Just let me know when I can return. By the way, you are?"

Pulling a card from his suit jacket pocket, he stated, "I am William Farnsworth, hired by Michael and Cecilia Hunter to represent Mr. Griggs."

"All right, sir. I will be out in the hallway."

After Duncan closed the room door, William Farnsworth put his briefcase on the floor and walked over to the bed. "Good morning. How are you doing this morning?"

"Ah, a little flabbergasted. Michael and Cecilia sent you here?"

"Yes, they did. They heard you were in trouble and thought you could use some help."

"Wow, miracles never cease to happen. You know they are my in-laws, or rather my ex-in-laws, due to my divorce?"

"Yes, I do. They told me all about you last night. I wish I had in-laws like yours."

"They have always stayed in touch with me, even after the divorce and I ended up on the street. I never really appreciated them as much as I should have."

"So, let's get down to business. I don't want to upset Officer Duncan any more than is necessary. Why don't you tell me what has happened so I can decide how to handle things?"

As Farnsworth pulled out a small recorder, I told him everything, beginning with the first night I helped Marcie with the gang members who had broken into her restaurant. I explained how I tried to help her, and in return, she fed me until the night they broke in again and assaulted her. Then, my anger took over, and I was out for retribution. I described how I stopped the first two gang members from committing several crimes. I admitted I went a bit too far by breaking all the bones in their hands, but I didn't want them to attack Marcie again.

"With the last three gang members, I discovered they had a stash of drugs in their small hideout at an old, abandoned grocery store. After I took the drugs and disposed of them, I decided to neutralize them, especially since I didn't expect the courts to do anything about it."

Farnsworth asked several questions, especially about the identities of the two stores where the gang members were committing crimes. He said he would need them as witnesses to credibly testify for me. I wasn't sure how he would handle my attack on the last three gang members.

"I believe we've kept Officer Duncan waiting long enough. I advise you not to answer any of his questions without your attorney present. I will provide him with information about the store owners who were assaulted by the gang members and will decide what additional details I think he should have. I will also leverage some influence with the police chief, whom I know quite well, so you can relax and recover."

"That sounds like a plan, sir."

"Good! I will get out of here and let Duncan in." With that, he tucked his recorder into his pocket, grabbed his briefcase, and smoothly slipped out of the room.

As Officer Duncan entered the room, his face reflected consternation.

"So, I guess, by the look on your face, Officer, that Mr. Farnsworth told you I would not be answering any questions?"

"You got that right. You sure you don't want to answer even a couple of questions?"

"I tell you what, Officer. You ask the questions, and I will decide which ones, if any, I will answer."

"That's a deal."

During the next fifteen or twenty minutes, Duncan asked around twenty questions, of which I only answered two. One was about my family and how to contact them. The other was about Marcie. He mentioned he suspected Marcie had strong feelings for me and wondered if I felt the same about her.

Wondering about the motives behind the question about Marcie, I asked, "Why would you ask me that? It sounds personal. Do you want a relationship with her?"

"I have been trying since I first met her the night her restaurant was broken into, but she kept turning me down. Then, just the other day, she agreed to go on a date with me. So, I just wanted to let you know."

As I thought about what Duncan just told me, I realized that maybe what I saw from Marcie was only sympathy, and there was no real connection. "Officer, if you're interested in her, go for it. I am not the right person to get involved with her. Look at me. I live on the street and might end up in jail. No. You go ahead."

"I appreciate that. Since you aren't answering my questions, I'll have to hand over what I have to the detectives and let them take it from there. I hope you recover. Wouldn't want you to end up in jail in your current condition."

"Gee, thanks, Duncan. Just for you, I will try to get better," I said with a bit of sarcasm.

After Duncan left, I started to regret giving my approval for him to date Marcie. Who was I to decide that? Wasn't that Marcie's decision? If she wanted to date him, then that was her choice. I felt it was unlikely anything would work out between Marcie and me anyway.

A nurse entered my room, checked all the monitoring equipment attached to me, rechecked my vitals, and then, after recording information on my chart, said, "You have improved dramatically since last night. We are going to move you out of the ICU and down to a regular ward. Additionally, several individuals, who appear unkempt, are waiting to see you. We can't let them in here, but in your new room, they can visit. Just take it easy, and when you get tired, kick everyone out."

Once in my new room, my first visitors were Rafe and Wolf. They showed genuine concern for me and, in their way, offered to help me in any way they could. This was meaningful, considering they were homeless, just like I was.

Already tired, I thanked them and asked them to return later, to which they agreed. As I lay my head back on my pillow, four new visitors approached my room: Marcie, Fran, Maxine, and one person in a wheelchair. Although he looked familiar, I couldn't quite place him.

"Hey there again, Joshua," Marcie said as she approached the bed and once again took my hand in hers. "How are ya doin'?"

"Got a little tired with a bunch of visitors."

"We won't stay long. We have someone here we would like you to meet. This is my brother, John. John, meet Joshua."

John, wheeling his chair up to the bed next to me, said, "Hey there, Cowboy. What's cookin'?"

My eyes widened like a hoot owl's as I stared at John. "What in the world! John! What are you doing here? Are you Marcie's brother? No! You gotta be kidding me!"

I leaned over to the side of the bed as far as my sore stomach would let me, and John leaned out of his chair. We shared big bear hugs, tears flowing down our faces. As we pulled apart, I wiped the tears off my face, shook my head, and said again, "You have got to be kidding me!"

After finally regaining my composure, I realized John had my hand in his grip. "You saved my life, brother. And it sounds like you also saved my sister's life. We owe you big time. If there's anything, and I mean anything, we can do for you, just say so."

I was speechless and overcome with emotion. I looked at Marcie, then at John, then at Marcie.

Marcie now spoke up. "Look, Joshua. We know you are tired, and you need your rest. I called Officer Duncan to let him know you were awake, so we will get out of here to give you some time to rest before he arrives."

Finally getting my voice back, I said, "Oh, he has already been here. Additionally, my ex-in-laws became aware of me and hired a lawyer to represent me. I don't know how they found out, but they have always kept close track of me, even after the divorce. I sure couldn't have afforded a high-priced lawyer like him."

"That is great. Now, we are getting out of your hair. Get some rest and recover. We have a lot to talk about," John said as he turned his chair and wheeled out the door with the rest of his family following him.

CHAPTER 22

I was awakened several times during the night to have my vitals checked, and the bandage on my wound was changed. I got some sleep in between visits, but when I woke up the next day, I didn't feel very rested. I hadn't eaten much for the past few days, so I was starving when breakfast arrived. I knew I needed to eat slowly so I wouldn't upset my stomach. Most of the food tasted somewhat bland, but I needed nourishment.

I heard a knock on the door as I finished what I could manage to eat, pushing my food tray away from the bed. When the door opened, a person I had never expected to see again, my ex-wife, Virginia, walked in. As she walked over to the bed, she took my hand softly, saying, "Oh, Joshua. What has happened to you?"

"Wow, Ginny. What a surprise, especially after the way I treated you."

"Despite all that, Joshua, I have always loved you. I couldn't live with you anymore and needed more than you had to offer. I'm so sorry. I hate to see you like this."

"Huh, you and me both, but I will recover. After that, I don't know what will happen to me. I have been involved in some things the police are interested in, but your parents have hired a lawyer for me, so tell them that I greatly appreciate it."

"I know. I know. That is how I found out you were shot and in the hospital. I know they have been keeping tabs on you."

"They have. They are wonderful people. I can't thank them enough for everything they've done for me, especially now."

"I will tell them. I must get to work now, but I just wanted to see you and let you know I am praying for your recovery."

"Thanks, Ginny."

Virginia now leaned down, placed one hand on my face, and kissed me on the cheek. Turning to leave the room, she stopped, turned back to me, and said, "I still love you."

As she exited the room, I saw Marcie standing by the doorway with a somewhat pained expression. "Marcie. Hi. Come in."

****

It was hard for Marcie to process what she had just seen and heard. Here was another woman who had just kissed Joshua and told him she loved him, and it definitely wasn't his mother. Her emotions churned in her stomach, and she started feeling sick. Without saying a word, she turned from the doorway and hurried down the hall, even as she heard Joshua call out for her as she left. She couldn't face him right now. Maybe not ever again.

****

I didn't understand what had happened. Marcie just ran away from me. Why? I didn't get it, especially after she showed me so much attention. Maybe there was a romantic relationship between her and

Officer Duncan. I was definitely no competition for him; that was for sure.

As I lay in my bed, getting more and more depressed by the minute, I was interrupted. "Looks like you are doing better," Doctor Hayes walked into the room and over to the bed. "How are you feeling?"

"Sore and a bit beat up, but not too bad considering. When can I get out of here?"

"Not for a few days, which is one of the reasons I came in to see you. Before your surgery last night, we performed an MRA because of a minor head wound you received. A bullet just grazed your skull, but we needed to make sure there wasn't any hidden interior damage. We found something strange."

"Oh, brother. What? Do I have a tumor or something?"

"No. Not at all. What we found was a tiny piece of what might be shrapnel lodged in your brain. It is resting alongside your amygdala. Have you had any angry outbursts, headaches, or anything else?"

I sat in dumb silence. Finally collecting myself, I answered, "All of the above. I have had some blackouts from the headaches at times. But after I was injured in Afghanistan, they checked me over completely. None of the VA doctors could figure out what was causing the anger management issues or the headaches."

"It is just a tiny piece and shows up as a tiny dot. It may have been in a position where VA X-rays or MRIs could not detect it. It may have moved to its current location. So, I have a question: do you want us to attempt to remove it? It is a delicate operation, and there is always the possibility we will do something with worse side effects for you."

"Doctor, my anger management issues caused me to lose my wife and most of my friends, and put me out on the street. I may even end up going to jail. So, I don't think anything you could do would cause me side effects any worse than what I have gone through with that piece of sh*t in my brain. So, let's not discuss it any further. Just do it."

"We must wait a few days for you to recover from your current injury."

"One problem is that it might prevent you from doing the surgery, Doc. I don't have the money to pay you. As I already said, I'm homeless. I might have a little money in the bank, but not enough for a surgery like that."

"Let me stop you right there. I was contacted by Michael Hunter, who inquired about paying your medical bills. I told him about the piece of shrapnel, and he said he's paying for anything you need. So, as soon as you've recovered a bit from the gunshot wound, we'll go ahead with the surgery. I'll let you know when that will be."

"Thank you so much, Doctor Hayes."

"Don't thank me yet. Please wait until we conduct a successful surgery. You can thank Mr. Hunter, though." Doctor Hayes then heard his name being paged; he excused himself and left the room.

Taking a deep breath, I let my mind flash back and forth to everything that had happened since last night. It was amazing how the Lord works in a believer's life. When one door seemed to close, another opened, and I saw the firsthand benefit of that.

There was another knock on the door before I could think of anything else. Miracles kept happening to me. In the doorway stood my mother, Karen Griggs. It had been months since I last saw her, and as much as I dearly loved her, I didn't want to inflict the pain I was feeling on her, especially after my father passed away. What I didn't realize was that my absence had caused her even more pain.

Holding out my arms to her, signaling that I wanted her to come to me, she rushed into the room and to my bedside with tears running down her face. Without saying a word, she hugged me tightly. Finally, when she had her emotions somewhat under control, she pulled back, wiping tears from her face. She sat on the edge of the bed for several minutes, studying me to refresh her memory.

"Considering all you have been through, my boy, you look pretty good."

"I probably look better than I feel. I still feel beat up, but that will improve. The doctor said I am going to recover completely." I told my mother about my recent conversation with the doctor regarding the piece of shrapnel in my brain, and once I recover from the gunshot wound, they plan to remove it. What I didn't tell my mother was that the surgery was very risky and could have some serious side effects. She was already worried enough.

My mother stayed with me, talking and holding my hand for an hour, but then, noticing that I was starting to doze off, she left to give me some time to rest. She felt she had reconnected with me and would have many more chances to spend time with her son in the future.

****

Back in her restaurant, Marcie threw herself into work to forget about Joshua. When her sister saw how distracted she was, she grabbed her by the shoulders, stopped her, and turned Marcie to face her. "What's going on with you today, sis? I thought you'd be feeling good and upbeat. You looked like someone had just crashed your tea party."

Realizing she could not get by without saying something, Marcie looked into her sister's eyes and said, "After we all went up to see Joshua, I went back to ask him some questions and tell him how I felt about him. But when I got there, a beautiful woman about his age held his hand and leaned over to kiss him. As she walked out, she turned to him and said she loved him."

"Maybe you misread the situation, sis."

"No. I don't think so. What was going on was pretty obvious. He has another woman in his life and was keeping that from me. I'm done. I'm not going to get hurt again." Marcie turned and went back to her work.

Fran approached her mom, who was also helping prepare the restaurant for the evening meal, and shared everything Marcie had told her. They understood Marcie would have to face this alone, but they always supported her whenever she needed it.

****

My attorney, William Farnworth, visited my room three days later with good news. "I've spoken with the owners of the two stores where you interfered with the criminal activity of those gang members. They couldn't identify you but said you saved them, especially the Indian store owner's daughter, from a terrible situation.

We can say that the thieves' broken hands happened only because you defended those store owners. The other three cases are somewhat different, but here's the situation. During my research, which included reviewing your background, I discovered that you received the Congressional Medal of Honor for your actions in Afghanistan, where you saved most of your unit and members of another unit. That will go a long way in considering your actions. I was also told that you still have a piece of shrapnel in your brain that likely caused you to behave the way you did. So, in the end, none of that was your fault. I spoke with the prosecutor about you, and he was hesitant to put a war hero on trial for something like this."

Farnsworth continued, "Bottom line, Joshua, there will be no charges, especially since the doctor just told me they are going to operate to remove that piece of metal in hopes it will give you a normal life again."

I lay stunned. It was hard for me to absorb all that Farnsworth had told me. "Sir, will you write all that down for me? I'm just having a little trouble understanding all of it. It would help if I could read it and take some time to absorb it."

"Of course. The only point you must remember is that you aren't going to jail."

"Okay, but some guy has been looking for me for several weeks. I don't know what that was about. Can you find out?"

"Already did. He was from the VA, and a new doctor reviewed old cases. He managed to spot that tiny piece of metal in your brain. He had been trying to find you to get you back into the VA hospital to try to remove it. He is relieved now that he knows you will have it done here. I spoke to him, and he sent his heartfelt apologies for the VA missing it in the first place."

All I could do was lie in bed and shake my head. If it hadn't been for Marcie running out on me, I'd have called today one of the best days of my life, but she has dampened everything else. At least I wasn't going to jail. That was a big deal.

CHAPTER 23

Since the hospital scheduled me for follow-up brain surgery, they kept me confined for ten days to aid my recovery from the gunshot wounds, but the day finally arrived for the surgery. A stack of papers was placed in front of me to sign, giving consent and explaining, in various ways, the risks of this type of surgery and possible side effects if something went wrong. I didn't care. I just wanted it done, hoping to move on with my life, even if that life was still out on the streets. I had plenty of friends out there.

Virginia's parents stopped by to wish me Godspeed. My best street friends, Wolf and Rafe, also came by and were happy about what was happening. Marcie, her mom, sister, and brother were the only people missing. Well, I didn't understand it, but that was life. If you want to make God laugh, tell him your plans. I chuckled at that thought.

From the time I entered the surgery room until I came back out, a good four hours had elapsed. It was going to be another hour or more before I would come out from under the anesthetic for the doctors to see if the surgery had been successful. Everyone who had come to wish me well was still in the visitors' waiting room.

While waiting, Michael and Cecilia Hunter engaged in long conversations with Rafe and Wolf, captivated by their war stories. Michael had been too busy building his fortune to serve in the military, but he held great respect for all those who had served.

Michael was the first to see the doctor emerge from the recovery room. As the doctor approached, everyone crowded around to hear the news.

"Okay, Doc. How did it go?"

"The surgery appeared to go well. We won't know if we made any mistakes for a while, but we believe we were successful. The piece of metal was slightly larger than we expected. During the MRI, we initially examined only a tiny end, no bigger than the point of a sharpened pencil, but once we accessed it, it measured 7 millimeters long. How that piece of metal managed to penetrate that far without causing significant damage is beyond me. If you believe in miracles, that definitely qualifies."

"Can we go in and see him?" Cecilia questioned.

"Yes, but wait until we move him to a room. It will only be another fifteen minutes or so. And please keep your visits short. He needs his rest."

All morning, traffic in and out of my room was nonstop, with only two people entering at a time. Finally, as attorney Farnsworth left, I closed my eyes and got some much-needed rest. The doctor had briefed me on the surgery, but until I was completely out from the anesthetics, neither they nor I would know how successful it was.

****

While Marcie was cleaning the dining room after the breakfast crowd had left, her phone rang. Her brother told her he had heard from Rafe, Joshua's friend, that he had recovered well from the surgery. However, it might be a day or two before they do tests to check for any harmful side effects from the surgery.

Marcie thanked John, then returned to her cleaning. Although she was glad to hear Joshua was okay, she knew she needed to forget about him. He had other interests, and she had to move on with her life. She even agreed to a dinner date with Officer Duncan scheduled for tomorrow night and was looking forward to a stress-free evening out.

"Who was on the phone, Marcie?" her mom asked as she came into the dining area to help Marcie clean up. "Was that about Joshua?"

"Yes, Mom. It was John. Joshua came through the surgery fine, but it will be a day or two before they know if he will completely recover from it."

"Aren't you going to go see him?" she queried.

"No, I don't see why I should. Joshua has another woman in his life; he will likely be with her if he returns to normal. I need to get on with my life. So, enough talk about that. We have work to do."

****

Over the next two days, I underwent comprehensive testing in every possible way, and no impairments were found. Doctor Hayes signed off on my file and said they would prepare me to go home in a few days. I wondered what returning home would mean. Could I go back with my mother? Would she want me to live with her again, or would I end up back on the streets? I had so many questions with no answers that I started to feel close to a panic attack.

Although I might stay with my mom for a while, I knew I would need to find a job and my own place, even if my personality had gone back to pre-Afghanistan days. I wasn't sure what kind of job I could handle, but I would have time to figure it out.

By the third day after the brain surgery, I was up, limping down the halls of the hospital, slowly at first as my legs were a bit weak, but each day, my strength improved. I also started to gain weight from consistent hospital meals, even though they lacked a bit of taste.

I learned there was a barbershop on the hospital's ground floor, so I convinced my nurse that I could go there for a haircut and beard trim. The nurse, however, insisted that I take the wheelchair, so I didn't wear myself out. I had agreed.

Although I didn't want my hair cut back to the military style, I had a lot of it cut off. It was down on my neck a bit and a little on my ears, except for where they had shaved the back of my head for the surgery. A hat would soon cover that until my hair grew back. The rest of my hair was pretty full, which I brushed back, leaving a slight, almost indistinguishable part in the middle.

My beard was a different story. I had worn it uncut for so long that I was worried about how I would see myself if I trimmed it all off. After talking with the barber, we agreed that my face could probably use a break from the hair, and any bugs, food, or other gunk that had built up over the months could be washed away. When he finished, I looked in the mirror and almost didn't recognize myself. From just below my eyes, the entire upper half of my face was dark brown and weathered. Below where the beard had been was a stark, pale white.

I still hadn't regained all my normal weight, so my face looked a bit thin, but part of that was due to the missing hair. I would have to eat more to regain a satisfactory weight. I did not want to go job hunting looking like this. Some good sunshine would improve my appearance and mood.

Under the doctor's orders, I had to leave the hospital in a wheelchair. I brought a few belongings, but I insisted on keeping most of the clothes I was wearing before I was shot, except for the blood stains, which my mother had worked very hard to clean and remove. She signed my discharge papers while I was dressed in the new clothes she had bought. As the nurse wheeled me out of the elevator toward the main entrance, my mother approached me with the discharge papers, her face marked by worry.

"What's the matter, Mom? Have they decided not to let me go?"

"That's not it, son. When I tried to pay for your care, I was told it had already been paid for. I know I couldn't have paid the whole amount, but I could have paid part."

"Oops. I suppose we forgot to mention this to you. Ginny's parents paid for everything."

"How could they do that? Why would they do that?"

"They could because they are loaded with money. They would because they have always loved me. You know that."

"I guess you are right. Even with the divorce?"

"Yes, even after the divorce. They occasionally reached out to me over the past few months to check on me. I had never had anger management issues when I was around them. It was just living at home with you, where you always saw me. I am so sorry, Mom, for all the trouble and heartache I caused you, especially after Dad died."

"I just had a hard time coping with all of that, son. I should have been more patient, but when I… we lost your dad, I was just so thin-skinned, and your behavior affected me more than it should have."

"No, Mom! It wasn't your fault. It was mine, and it was out of my control. It isn't anymore. Can I come back to the house for a little while until I figure out what to do? I will work hard to be the best son you could have."

"I know you will, Joshua, and we can head back to the house. That's where I was planning to take you anyway. It will give you a chance to heal and fully stabilize your life. You know you have a pretty big bank account."

"How can that be, Mom?"

"As a recipient of the Congressional Medal of Honor, you receive over $2,200 a month for life. You've already had more than $12,000 in your account since you and Ginny didn't spend much while you were on active duty. When she divorced you, she thought you would need that money, so she didn't take a penny. That shows how much she loved you. Last I checked, you had over $37,000."

"Wow. Why didn't I realize that?"

"You had other issues to worry about, and you became so angry, so easily, that it took up all your time and energy. But, now, let's see how things go."

"Do you think there is any chance Ginny would come back to me after all this time, Mom?"

My mom took my hands in hers. She realized no one had told me my wife had remarried several months earlier. The burden was on her, and she didn't enjoy having to be the one to tell me, but she knew she had no other choice.

"Son, I am sorry to be the bearer of bad news, but Ginny remarried a few months ago. I'm so sorry. As much as she loved you, she needed someone who would love and support her and be there when she needed someone."

Although I looked at my mother grimly as I considered what I had just heard, I realized she was right. "I understand, Mom. Seeing her the other day was good, and she looked happy. That is what is important. I still love her, but she has moved on with her life, as I should. I wish her the best."

The nurse behind the desk handed Karen extra paperwork for her after-surgery instructions. "You are free to go," she said. Turning toward Joshua, she instructed him, "Inside the envelope are medical guidelines, wound care instructions, and phone numbers to call if you have any questions. If you develop a fever or experience any other issues, return here right away. And, thank you for your service, Marine."

After acknowledging her thanks, I turned my wheelchair around and told my mother, "Let's get out of here and go home."

"We are on our way. Do you want home cooking or some Kentucky Fried Chicken?"

"I want your home cooking. I've missed that more than anything else, even though the food I got from Marcie's restaurant was really good."

Mom rolled me out to the curb, where her car was waiting. "Who is Marcie, and what restaurant are you talking about?"

"Oh, that's not important. We can talk about it later." Climbing into my mom's car and handing the wheelchair to the nurse who followed us out, I settled in and snapped on my seatbelt. Marcie was history, and I hoped my mom wouldn't remember to ask me about her. My hopes went unanswered.

CHAPTER 24

While I was sitting in a chair at the small kitchen table, my mom donned an apron and moved from cabinet to cabinet, gathering the ingredients for dinner.

"Mom, don't do anything fancy. Just a burger or something would be great."

"Not on your life, and not on your first night home. I don't know how many months it has been, but I am going to fix you a decent meal, just like I remember your favorite."

"Beef Stroganoff? Really, Mom, you don't have to go to that trouble."

"It's no trouble. You can have a burger tomorrow night. I will do right by you tonight, as I should have been doing all these months. So, sit and tell me about this, Marcie."

Oh no! She remembered. I didn't want to go over the whole story, but I knew I couldn't stay silent. "Okay, Mom. Just the short version of it, okay?"

"Okay, and don't think I'm not listening while I cook. I am."

Of course she is, I thought. "It has been several weeks, but one night, I was rummaging through a dumpster for something to eat when…"

"You were what?" she shouted as she turned toward me from the sink.

"Now, Mom, will you let me tell this story?"

"Okay, okay. I will keep my trap shut until you finish, and then you will hear from me."

"As I was saying, I was looking for food when a young woman named Marcie came out of the alley door and offered me a meal. After I ate and was leaving, some thugs broke into her restaurant and assaulted her. You know how angry and reckless I was when I was home after returning from Afghanistan. I jumped into the fight and managed to take down three of them, but a fourth hit me from behind. Marcie managed to knock him out with a chair. I left before the police arrived. For several weeks, I went there at night for a meal and agreed to stay overnight as a security guard. One night, I was late because I was helping a veteran friend of mine. When I arrived at the restaurant, those guys had broken in again and beaten her up. It turned out she had shot one of them."

I paused to let what I said sink in. Then I continued, "My anger got the best of me. I found out who they were and went after them. I took out two of them, but when I targeted the others, one of them shot me. That's how I ended up in the hospital. You know the rest."

By this time, Mom had stopped her dinner preparations and leaned against the kitchen counter with her mouth hanging open. Now, after overcoming her shock, she said, "If you hadn't told me that story yourself, I wouldn't believe it, but I know you don't lie." Walking around the counter, she approached me and gave me a hug. "I'm so proud of you, son, and I know your father looks down on you, feeling the same way."

"To be honest, Mom, I didn't have any more control over my emotions than when I returned from Afghanistan, and I don't know if the surgery corrected that issue."

Standing back up and resuming her dinner preparations, she said, "So tell me more about this, Marcie."

"Well, she is a lovely young woman who also served as a Marine. She has a brother who was deployed in Afghanistan; it turns out he was in my unit and was in my Humvee when it hit the IED. He lost both legs in the blast but appears to be doing well. I met Marcie's mother and sister at the restaurant. They all seemed like genuinely nice people."

"So, do you have feelings for this young lady? The expressions on your face when you talk about her make it seem like you do, but I also notice some sadness there."

"I thought I did, Mom, and she might have feelings for me, but I was a street person, so I probably got it wrong. I think she's involved with a police officer. I saw her talking to him once, and I believe she's dating him. She's not going to pick me over someone like that."

"Based on what you've told me, it sounds like she was showing you some compassion, and maybe there was more than you initially thought. You should act on that if you still have feelings for her."

"I'm not ready to be back in the game and certainly not ready to compete against a police officer. I don't even know her last name. So, let's drop it there."

"Okay. One last question: why did she have a restaurant in that poor part of town where you spent so much of your time?"

"She said she only wanted to help people who are less fortunate than she is. She typically served two affordable meals each day that low-income families could afford. Many of them even showed up one morning to help clean up and repair the damage caused by those thugs."

"Okay, I need to get this food going. Thank you, son, for sharing that with me. If I don't get busy, we might starve to death."

"Not to worry, Mom. I have been a lot hungrier than this."

"Oh, by the way, I saw a couple of your veteran buddies in the hospital, so I invited them for dinner tonight. I hope that is all right."

"Oh, that is just fine, Mom. I hope they have cleaned up because they live on the street. But at least they could spend the night in homeless shelters, unlike me, who got kicked out of all of them because of my anger issues."

"Not a problem. We will take them however they show up."

The doorbell rang as my mom finished preparing the stroganoff, setting the table, and placing the food in serving bowls.

"I will get that, Mom." As I went to the door, I was still limping from my old leg injury, which I hadn't considered in a while. I looked out the peephole and then opened the door to welcome Rafe and Wolf. Wolf was helping pull Rafe's wheelchair up the two steps on the front porch.

"Sorry about that, guys. My house isn't designed for chairs."

"Not a problem," Wolf said. "I got him."

Finally, I entered the house and took my two friends into the kitchen, where my Mom was waiting for them.

"Thanks for coming, boys. Scoot up to the table and dig in."

"Thank you so much for this, ma'am."

As I helped my mom into a chair, I sat down and said, "Let us pray." Reaching out, we clasped each other's hands, and I prayed, "Bless us, oh Lord, for these gifts which we are about to receive from Your bounty through Christ our Lord." I crossed myself, saying, "In the name of the Father, Son, and the Holy Spirit. Amen. Let's eat."

****

Throughout dinner, Karen felt grateful and relieved to have her son back, and she enjoyed chatting with Rafe and Wolf. She subtly managed to get Rafe to reveal Marcie's restaurant name. She had some ideas about what she wanted to do, but wasn't ready to share them yet. She decided to wait and see how things played out first.

While loading the dishwasher, she told Joshua that she needed to do some shopping the next day, but he had to stay home and continue recovering from his surgery. He happily agreed, admitting he was tired and didn't want his friends to leave, but he needed to go to bed.

Although she didn't have much space, Karen offered Rafe and Wolf the chance to stay overnight. They thanked her and said they were already prepared for the night. They also expressed gratitude for the delicious meal and the bags of fruit she insisted they take. After they left, Joshua gave his mother a hug and a kiss before heading to bed.

Karen still had a few things to do before she hit the hay. Taking her cell phone out of her purse, she went to Google and typed in "Marcie's Outpost." The restaurant's name, a photo of its front, and a map pinpointing its location appeared. Writing the address down on a paper pad, she ripped the sheet off and stuck it into her purse.

Now, it was her bedtime, as she had a busy day tomorrow that included lunch at a particular restaurant.

CHAPTER 25

Bright light streaming through my bedroom window finally woke me from a deep sleep. Turning away from the light, I looked at the clock on the nightstand. I guess I needed the sleep, I thought. It's eleven o'clock.

Sitting up against my pillows, I gently stretched to check my pain level and found it wasn't too bad. Reaching up and touching my head where the surgeon had gone in to remove a piece of shrapnel, I winced a little since that area was still sore to the touch, as was my stomach where I had been shot.

Standing up, I moved around a bit and realized that although I was sore, I wasn't experiencing any sharp pains. It was nothing I couldn't handle. Even though the sun was shining brightly, it was still a little cool inside the house, so I slipped into a pair of slippers and pulled my robe off the back of the closet door. I headed into the bathroom to finish my morning routine.

As I left the bathroom, I heard no other sounds in the house. Although I suspected my mom might have already gone out to do her shopping, I still called her name as I entered the kitchen. There was no answer, but a note on the fridge showed she had gone shopping and would return at lunchtime. It also said that my breakfast was in the oven for me to heat up.

An orange in a bowl on the counter looked especially good, so I peeled it for breakfast. Once I was fully awake, I would likely feel hungry.

Walking around the house, I noticed that not much had changed since my last visit. My mother had turned my dad's small office into a craft room where she sewed, made greeting cards, and possibly more. The rest of the house stayed the same, as neat as ever, with everything in its place.

After peeling the orange, I threw the peels in the trash. Then, leaning over the sink, I separated the pieces and enjoyed the orange's sweet, tangy flavor. Before leaving the hospital, the nurse told me to take a shower but to try to keep the surgical sites as dry as possible.

I found waterproof bandages in my mother's bathroom medicine cabinet, so I used them before taking a shower. I had a patch of hair missing where the surgery had been, but I knew I could hide it with my Stetson—if I still had it. It had been with me through a lot, and I hoped it had been recovered.

After the shower, I found a set of clothes on a chair in my room that my mother had left out for me. The Levi's and Western-style shirts generally fit, but I don't fill them out as well as I used to. A little extra weight would fix that.

When I was fully dressed, I heated my pancakes, sausage, and hashbrowns for breakfast. As I sat at the table eating, I heard the front door unlock. Turning around, I saw my mother struggling with several plastic grocery bags. Getting up from my chair as quickly as my injuries allowed, I went over to help her with the bags.

"Mom, it would be better if you had left this stuff in the car and had me bring it in. I'm not an invalid."

"You don't need to be carrying a bunch of stuff. Remember what the doctor said. You need to take it easy for at least a week."

"I know, but I had a good night's sleep, almost finished your wonderful breakfast, and I have a couple of small errands to run today."

"I don't think you should be going out already."

"I promise not to overdo it. I will be back in about an hour. Do you have a list of taxis? I'm not up to driving yet."

"Yes, I do, and that is very sensible. I could certainly drive you."

"Thank you, Mom, but I can do this alone." I went to the hall closet, rummaged through it, and found a black leather jacket that had once belonged to my father. I slipped my arms into the sleeves; it fit, though a little large on me, just like the rest of my clothes, but it would work. I then returned to my mom, hugged her gently, kissed her on the cheek, and said, "Be back in a bit."

****

Karen was happy to have this time to herself. Her little trip that morning was very productive. She went to the grocery store to stock up on food for her son. After she finished her shopping, she pulled the slip of paper containing the name and address of Marcie's restaurant out of her purse and headed that way. She was surprised to find the restaurant in a plain neighborhood, where many shops were closed, and there were no signs of wealth. She did wonder why Marcie would choose a location in such a rundown area.

As Karen parked across the street from the restaurant, she sat for a minute to watch. Some people came and went from the restaurant, primarily families whose clothes had seen better days. Everyone who left seemed to have smiles or happy expressions, especially the children, so they sure seemed to be satisfied customers. She decided it was time to find out who this Marcie person was.

Exiting her car and shutting the door, Karen made sure it was locked, hoping to keep her groceries safe. She then crossed the street, holding the door open for a mother and her two young children to enter ahead of her.

Her first impression was positive. The restaurant's interior was clean and brightly colored, with crayons and paper visible on several tables where children sat. The place was about half full, so she quickly found an empty table. There was no sign indicating that she needed to wait to be seated.

Within a minute, a charming woman who seemed about her age approached her table with a glass of water and a menu. "Would you like something else to drink besides water? Coffee or tea, ma'am?"

"Coffee would be nice with cream and sugar. What is this 'ma'am-stuff'? We are close in age. My name is Karen."

Laughing, the woman introduced herself as Maxine. She explained that she believed in showing respect to all customers, regardless of their financial conditions, because she values each one of them.

"I see. Okay. Thank you, Maxine. Am I too late for breakfast, or is it lunchtime?"

"We only serve two meals a day: breakfast and an early dinner. We can still get you something for breakfast. But first, if you don't mind me asking, you are dressed a little too nicely for this neighborhood?"

"Yes, I guess I am. I just heard about your restaurant and wanted to see what all the hullabaloo was about."

"Well, that is nice. Who did you hear it from?"

Karen did not want to reveal her true purpose, so she simply said she had seen something on the news about it. As Maxine went to get her coffee, Karen started looking for someone who might be Marcie. She spotted a young woman who seemed too young to be the person Joshua had described. Eventually, as more customers left and Karen was alone, an attractive blonde with her hair up in a bun at the back of her head entered the dining area and sat at a table with a cup of coffee. She wore a very stained apron, so she was probably the cook.

She wondered whether this was Marcie, the owner, or just the cook, and whether the owner was even there today. As Maxine returned with Karen's coffee, she took a sip and said, "This is delicious coffee. Did you make it, and what kind is it?"

"No. I didn't. Marcie over there made it this morning, but I don't recall what kind it is. I will go ask her."

"That's all right. Don't bother her. She looks tired."

With that opening, Karen asked Maxine why Marcie was so tired. Maxine sat at Karen's table with only a few other customers to serve and began telling the story about Marcie, the gang members, and how a street person named Joshua had stepped in to help. As Maxine described how Joshua had chased after the gang members to detain them and prevent them from bothering Marcie, Karen noticed Marcie getting up from her table and walking toward her.

"Mom, I can hear what you're saying. You don't need to keep going on about all that's happened. I'm sure this woman has better things to do."

"That's all right, Marcie. It is fascinating. I'm Karen, by the way." They shook hands, and then Karen asked, "So this guy had been living on the street, and he helped you out? That is amazing."

"That he did. I probably wouldn't be standing here now if it weren't for him."

"If I may be nosy, what has happened to him?"

Hesitating, unsure if she wanted to continue the story, Marcie finally said, "He got shot while going after the last three gang members and ended up in the hospital. It was a close call, but he survived."

"Wow, what a story. Have you gone up to see him and thank him?"

Reluctantly, Marcie kept going. "Yes, I was up there, but then another beautiful woman showed up, and they seemed connected, so I did not want to impose."

Karen kept trying to find ways to ask questions without tipping off Marcie about why she was asking. "Oh, so is he married, and was that his wife?"

"I don't think he is married," Maxine chimed in. "Marcie isn't sure either. Marcie's husband was killed in Iraq a few months ago. I thought for a while that a spark was igniting between them, but now Marcie says there isn't."

"Mom, there's another woman in his life. She was beautiful, and I wouldn't dare compete with her. Besides, he has anger management issues, and I don't think he's fully interested in me. He's also homeless, living on the street."

"No, he's not..." Karen started to say, realizing she wasn't supposed to know any of this information, so she stopped.

With a questioning look, Marcie looked at Karen, asking, "He's not what?"

Stumbling over her words, Karen finally blurted out, "I meant to say that just because he is homeless and lives on the street does not mean he is not a good person."

"That is true. He did seem to be a sincere and caring person." She then turned to her daughter. "Right, Marcie?"

"You are right, Mom, but enough of this conversation. It is in the past. We have work to do to get ready for dinner this afternoon. It was nice meeting you, Karen. We hope to see you here again."

After finishing her meal, Karen left the table and went back to the kitchen counter. She then opened her purse, took out a hundred-dollar bill, and placed it on the table for the bill and tip. It was the least she could do, but she had already decided it wasn't all she would do.

****

"Mom, why did you tell that strange woman that story?"

"She seemed nice, and she saw you looked tired, and when I told her you were, because of all that had happened, the story started coming out. I'm sorry. I probably shouldn't have."

"No. It's okay, Mom."

After cleaning Karen's dishes, Fran came back from the dining room. "Look at this!" she exclaimed. She was holding a hundred-dollar bill. "This is what that customer left on the table. Can you believe that?"

"That is strange," Maxine commented. "But she was dressed well and better than most of our customers. That certainly puts us over the top in terms of income over expenses for today. I wonder who she is?"

"Probably just a curious, wealthy person trying to satisfy her curiosity."

"Enough, already. Let's get back to work," Marcie directed.

CHAPTER 26

When I arrived at the First National Bank of Washington, I stepped out of the cab I had called and crossed the sidewalk to the front door. According to my mother, this is where I had an account. Unfortunately, I forgot to get my account number from her, so I couldn't access it. I had some identification, including my VA card and an old, unexpired driver's license. I found them in the dresser drawer at my mother's house.

Walking up to the cashier window, I said good morning to the pleasant-looking teller, who smiled from ear to ear.

"Good morning, sir. How can I help you?"

"Well, that big smile is a good start. How can anyone have a bad day after seeing that smile on your face?"

Blushing, the teller managed to thank me.

"I have been away for a while and not very active on my account. I want to find out the balance and make a withdrawal."

"I can do that for you, sir. If I could get your account number."

"Hmm, there is a little problem there. I don't remember it, and I don't have an old deposit slip or any other documentation with the number. I do have my ID, however. Can you look it up with that?"

"Oh, of course."

I withdrew my wallet, pulled out my ID, and then handed it through the window to the teller. As she clicked the keys on her computer, she finally looked up at me and stated, "With the most recent deposit, you have $38,452.76."

"Great. Hmm. Then I would like to withdraw $11,000."

"Wow, that is a big withdrawal. Do you want it in a check or cash?"

"Please give me $1,000 in cash. If you don't mind, in the fifties and twenties, then the rest in a check."

"That is fine. It will take me a few minutes."

While the teller handled my request, I moved to a small table with a coffee pot and donuts. I couldn't remember the last time I'd had a donut. I poured myself a cup of coffee with a little sugar and, using a napkin, picked up two bear claws. Sitting in a nearby chair, I slowly sipped my coffee and ate the savory donuts, dunking them into my coffee. Even though I had just finished breakfast earlier, the donuts were fantastic. I figured I needed to put on some more weight anyway.

As I finished my coffee and donuts, wiping my hands with a napkin, I glanced toward the teller handling my request to see if she was ready. An individual was standing in front of her, but I could see a wild look on the teller's face and in her eyes. Her eyes then flicked to me, back to the person in front of her, and then over to me again. This did not look good. First, she should have had a smile on her face if everything was okay. Second, this man should have been sent to a different teller, since this teller should have been busy with my transaction.

How did I get into these messes? It seemed like trouble followed me everywhere. Sadly for me, but luckily for the bank, I couldn't just let this slide. Dropping my paper coffee cup and napkin into a trash can near my seat, I slowly got up and approached the teller and the man standing in front of her. When I reached the counter, I looked at the customer and saw part of a mask covering his lower face. Without giving the man a chance to react, I swung my right leg, hitting him behind the knees and causing him to fall onto the tile floor. I then landed on top of him, pinning his arms to his sides because I didn't know if he had a weapon.

A security guard standing at an exit leaped into action as he saw the struggle and rushed over to me. "What is happening here?"

"Bank robber," I managed to shout out as I kept holding onto the man's arms.

Kneeling, the security guard helped me take the man's hands out of his pockets and behind his back. As they did, a small black revolver dropped onto the tile floor.

Now kneeling on the robber's back, I caught my breath and realized I had some pain in my stomach. The doctor wasn't going to like this. I was supposed to be taking it easy. I hoped I hadn't torn out any stitches. That wouldn't be good, but I wasn't going to let this guy get away with robbing the bank.

I heard someone on the phone calling 911. As I knelt there, I suddenly realized I had not acted out of anger. Yes, I was angry, but I kept my anger in check and responded carefully. It was enough proof to me that the surgery to remove the piece of shrapnel was a success.

After the police arrived and took statements from me and a few others inside the bank, they left with the bank robber, who was handcuffed between two officers. Amid all the excitement, I remembered I still had my money to get. Walking over to the shaken teller, I said, "Good job, ma'am. Giving me that look was the right thing to do."

"I didn't know what else to do. You looked like you could handle yourself, but the security guards were not in my line of sight. He made me keep my hands on the counter so I couldn't activate the silent alarm."

"Well, it all worked out fine. When you're ready, could you please complete my transactions? I have some other errands to do."

"Oh, yes. Of course." Putting down her glass of water, she methodically completed my request, handing me the check and the cash in a large envelope.

"Thank you so much for your help today."

"I'm sure the bank manager would like to talk to you. Thank you, too."

"I am in a hurry and don't want to be late for a doctor's appointment. Thank you." I then turned and walked out of the bank. I needed to find another taxi to get to my next stop. Looking across the street, I saw the same taxi that had taken me to the bank, so I walked across the street and got in.

"What happened over there?" the cab driver asked, turning around to look at me.

"Oh, not much. It's just some guy with an ill-conceived plan of trying to rob the bank. The police took care of him." I then gave the driver, who sat with his eyes wide open and mouth agape, the address of my next errand.

Ten minutes later, the cab driver stopped in front of the St. Vincent homeless shelter. It was one of the shelters I had been kicked out of twice and eventually banned from because of the trouble I caused each time I was there. Usually, it wasn't my fault. I was stopping other homeless individuals from being abusive to other residents in the shelter. Even though I had been kicked out, I knew they did good work and were especially helpful to all veterans, at least to those who were not disruptive.

Walking in the front door, I approached the first person who appeared to be a volunteer. "Good afternoon, ma'am. Could you direct me to the manager of this fine establishment?"

"He is quite busy. Maybe I can help you."

I knew no one there would recognize me, but I still wanted to speak with the manager himself. "No, ma'am. I need to talk with the manager. I have a large donation I would like to make."

"Oh. All right. I will see if he can break free."

Several minutes later, a tall, middle-aged man with a mostly bald head and a little too many donuts around his middle came out of a back room. As he walked toward me, I remembered the manager's name.

"Good afternoon, sir. How can I be of help?"

"George. I guess you don't remember me," I said, sticking my hand out. George stuck his hand out, and we shook.

"No, you don't look familiar."

Not surprising. I looked quite different the last few times you kicked me out of here. My name is Joshua Griggs. Does that ring a bell now?

"My God. I do remember your name and all the problems you caused here, but you appear to have changed."

"Yes, sir, I have, and I harbor no resentment toward your shelter. You did what was necessary for the well-being of the other occupants. I know you assist many veterans, so thank you for your efforts. Please make good use of this for my friends." I handed the $10,000 check to George, then turned and left through the door. My cab was still waiting for me.

****

Taking a short break after preparing for the dinner crowd, Marcie sat at a table in the dining area with a mug of hot chocolate. The weather had turned cold and damp, with some snowflakes drifting down that melted as they hit the sidewalk. After spending so much time in the desert of Afghanistan, Marcie loved the snow. She rose from the table, returned to the kitchen, grabbed her jacket, then walked back through the dining area and out the front door. She lifted her face to the sky, letting the snowflakes land on her face. She felt like she could do this all day. She enjoyed the outdoors more than being inside.

She heard a beep behind her as she prepared to go back to the restaurant. Turning around, she saw a police car approaching, and as it pulled over to the curb, she recognized Officer Duncan. Their dinner date a few nights ago had gone well, but Marcie didn't feel any real connection to him. He was easy to talk to, and they shared their life stories, but beyond that, there was no spark. She suspected he would ask her out again.

He greeted her as he exited his patrol car and walked toward her. "Good afternoon, Marcie. What are you doing standing out in this weather?"

"I love the snow. It is so much more pleasant than the desert and sand."

"Okay. If you say so." He stepped closer and took her hand. "I was hoping you had a good enough time the other night to agree to dinner again. I was thinking of tomorrow night."

As Marcie hesitated, Officer Duncan realized the date might not go through. "Have you changed your mind, Marcie? I can wait if you're busy. We can do it another night or have breakfast after I get off shift."

Finally, having found her voice and made her decision, she responded. "I'm sorry, but I don't think I will make it. I'm just not ready to start dating again so soon after my husband's death." It wasn't the complete truth, but close enough. She just wasn't up to dating him. Even though it appeared Joshua was dating that blonde, he was still too much on her mind.

"Maybe sometime in the future, but don't wait on me. I am a fickle woman, so I may never decide to date again."

"That would be a big loss, but I get it. You've been through a lot these past few weeks. Anyway, please keep me in mind. I'll keep checking on your restaurant from time to time. Is that okay?"

"That is fine. Thank you. I did purchase a video surveillance system to check the restaurant's status on my phone from home, so I feel better about everything now."

"That's great. I had better get back on patrol. You take care, Marcie. Be seeing you."

As Officer Duncan returned to his car, Marcie turned around and reentered her restaurant. She knew it probably disappointed him, but he would get over it. He was attractive, and she doubted he'd have trouble finding someone else.

****

I had decided to let my taxi take a quick drive-by past Marcie's restaurant, but I wasn't sure if I would stop to say hello. As the cab neared the restaurant, I saw a police car parked along the curb. Then I saw Officer Duncan on the sidewalk near Marcie, holding her hand. "Don't stop," I told the driver. "It's time for me to head home." This event just confirmed that Marcie was involved with the police officer. I needed to get her out of my head and move on with my life.

CHAPTER 27

When I returned to my mother's house, I saw her car in the driveway. My plan now was to focus on fixing things around the house that had been neglected since my father passed away. Walking into the house, I hung my dad's leather jacket on a hall tree and continued into the kitchen. My mom was at the stove cooking.

"What ya up to, Mom?"

She turned toward me with a big smile. "I thought, with this change in weather, some good spicy chili would go well. What do you think?"

"Sounds like a good idea. Once you've finished that, I would like to get a list of repairs that need to be done around here. I'm sure there are many, so I plan to spend the next few days addressing those tasks. I can go to the hardware store with the list and buy the necessary supplies. Also, I noticed some newspapers on the coffee table. I will review those and look at job offers. I need to get back out there to support myself."

"Now, son. Don't be in too much of a hurry. Remember, you need to recover first. Oh, by the way, while you were out, the bank manager at First National Bank—I believe that's the one where your account is—called and wanted to speak with you. Before he hung up, he expressed his gratitude, as well as that of all his employees, for your help today. What was that about?"

"No big deal. I just helped them with a minor issue involving one of their customers. Nothing worth mentioning." I never liked the attention I got for things I did for others. It wasn't in me to showcase those things for everyone to see. At least now, no anger was involved, and I wasn't upsetting people around me, other than an occasional bank robber.

My mother looked pleased with my explanation, so she went back to the chili on the stove. I grabbed a beer from the fridge and headed into the living room to see if I could find anything to watch on TV. Since I had been out on the streets for several months, most of what was on TV was probably of some interest.

As I scrolled through the channels, I stopped on the news channel. *Wow, where did they get that picture?* I thought to myself. My picture was on the TV, in uniform, and I could hear the reporter talking about the bank robbery attempt. Unfortunately, my mother had excellent hearing.

"What's that about, son? Was there a bank robbery today?" she asked as she walked into the living room. Then, seeing my picture on the TV, she added, "Is that what you were talking about when you said you helped the bank? You stopped a robbery?"

"Yeah, but it was no big deal. It wasn't dangerous or anything like that, and I had help from the security guards."

"How did you do it? Aren't you still hurting from the surgery?"

"Only a little. I checked my stitches, and they are fine. As I said, it was no big deal."

"You do seem to find trouble around you, but you also handle it well. You might want to consider applying to be a police officer.

Although that might put you back in the line of fire, and that would make me nervous."

"You've gone through enough stress over the past couple of years. I don't need to add to that. However, I'm unsure what kind of job I can get. I will have to be flexible. I didn't think about law enforcement, but I won't completely rule it out." *Although my bum leg probably would,* I thought.

After finishing my beer, I realized the day had worn me out, so I lay down for a short nap before dinner. I'd go to the hardware store tomorrow, buy the supplies I needed for any house repairs my mom required, and then start job hunting. But for now, it was nap time.

****

As Marcie reentered her restaurant, Fran approached her. "Was that Officer Duncan out there you were talking and holding hands with?"

"Yes, it was. He wanted to set another dinner date, but I told him I was not ready to start dating again. The other night, I had a good time, but we didn't have that spark or connection. He is a nice enough person, but just not the person for me."

"You could go out with him a few times just to see. Sometimes, that spark doesn't happen right away."

"He does seem like a nice guy, although I didn't think so the first couple of times I met him. And he is good-looking with a stable job, but I'm just not ready." Seeing Fran was about to say something else, Marcie interrupted her. "And enough about Joshua. I told you that it's probably a dead issue."

"Now that is some improvement. The last time we talked about him, you didn't use the word 'probably.' You seemed more certain before than you do now. What has changed?"

"Nothing has changed. I realize I miss him being around, even though he was dirty and stinky. He was a good person, but with those headaches and anger issues, I'm not sure we could have any relationship, especially with that blonde in his life."

"You know, you don't know anything about that blonde. You should contact him and ask him about her. That would help you make a better, more informed decision."

"You're probably right, but I don't know where to find him. He might even be back on the street. I could check some homeless shelters to see if someone can direct me to his location. But I've got too much on my plate, and I've been putting the burden of running the restaurant on you two, which isn't fair. I need to step up my game and take on more of the workload. It's my restaurant, after all."

The discussion about Joshua and Marcie's restaurant finally petered out as customers began entering the restaurant in search of a good evening meal. They all had to get back to work now.

****

While I was napping, my mother was planning her next move. She wanted me to have a few more days to recover and focus on house repairs, so I wouldn't suspect what she truly had in mind. She hoped and prayed I wouldn't be upset with her. She was confident that everything would be forgiven if things went as she hoped. However, she thought I might get upset if it didn't work out. It was a risk she was willing to take.

Valor in the Darkness

****

The next few days passed without incident, and neither Joshua nor Karen mentioned Marcie's name or discussed her restaurant. Saturday arrived, and she discovered that Marcie closed her restaurant only on Sunday to observe the Lord's Day of Rest. She had already talked to Joshua about going to Saturday night Mass, followed by dinner. He agreed but insisted on paying for the meal. She agreed but said she would choose the restaurant. When he asked her where they were going, she smiled and said it was a surprise, but the food was good.

As Saturday evening rolled around, Joshua asked his mom if wearing a coat and tie to Mass would be nice enough for the restaurant they were going to. She smiled and said it would be perfect.

Mass was at 6 p.m., and Karen knew from her conversations with Maxine that the restaurant did not take reservations; it was on a first-come, first-served basis, but it would be open when they arrived.

Karen and Joshua walked down the steps from church after Mass. "That was so refreshing and uplifting. I need to get back into the regular habit of it. With how I have lived for the past months, I would have been embarrassed to walk into a church, but I have missed it."

"That's good to hear, son. I am starving, so let's head to the restaurant." Just as they reached their car, Joshua held the door open for his mother, and the overcast sky opened up, sending a downpour of rain on them. Joshua had gotten wet before getting around the car and inside.

"Boy, that came out of nowhere." Taking his wet Stetson, which he had recovered from the hospital, he dropped it into the back seat to dry off. "OK, our next destination is the restaurant, but you need to tell me where we are going?"

"Just follow my directions, son."

Traffic was light, so it took them only 15 minutes to reach Marcie's restaurant. Joshua remarked that the area looked familiar and couldn't understand what kind of nice restaurant would be in this part of town, not even considering Marcie's.

Finally, Karen signaled for Joshua to pull over to the curb. "We are here. Would you bring me an umbrella from the back seat and hold it over me?" She was trying to distract Joshua from seeing where they would eat.

****

I threw my Stetson back on, even though it was drooping from the rain. I grabbed an umbrella, walked around the car, opened the door for my mom, and then held the umbrella for her as she stepped out.

As she took my arm and guided me across the street, I wasn't aware that the umbrella partly hid the restaurant's name. When we reached the curb, we stepped up and headed toward the front door. I reached out to open the door for my mom and led her inside. Then I turned my back to the restaurant to shake off the umbrella outside before going back in.

I hung the umbrella, hat, and rain jacket on a coat rack inside the door. Turning to find my mother, I saw she had already gone to a table and sat down. It took me a moment to realize what I was seeing. My mother was sitting at a table, and Maxine, Marcie's mom, was standing and talking with her.

Looking around the restaurant, it finally hit me hard, like a two-by-four to the head. This was Marcie's restaurant. I didn't see Marcie, but I saw Fran leave the kitchen and walk over to my mother's table. Then, from the corner of the dining room, her brother appeared. He was no longer in his wheelchair; now he sat in a regular chair, revealing his legs. I quickly realized he had prosthetics as he stood up and, a little unsteadily, walked toward me.

"Hey, brother. How's it going?" John grabbed me in a huge hug, and I reciprocated.

"What is going on here, John? It's good to see you, but this is a surprise."

Leaning close to my ear, John whispered, "I probably shouldn't be telling you this, but your mother has been a busy lady."

I pulled back from John. "She has now, has she?" Catching a movement out of the corner of my eye, I looked toward the kitchen. Marcie was standing with a dish towel in her hands, wearing a puzzled look on her face.

****

"What is going on out here?" she asked. Walking over to the table where Fran was talking to Karen, she continued. "It is nice to see you again, Karen. However, something is happening that I am not aware of. Who is that over there with my brother?" Marcie had not recognized Joshua without his long hair, beard, and street clothes.

Karen then stood and took Marcie's hands. "Marcie, I have been a bit deceptive. My name is Karen, but my full name is Karen Griggs."

Marcie looked at Karen and then back at her brother, who was standing with that strange man. But then, something about him seemed very familiar. Turning back to Karen, she said, "Griggs. That is Joshua's last name. Are you related to him?"

"I am his mother, and he is that man standing over there with your brother, just in case you didn't recognize him all cleaned up."

Marcie just stood staring at her brother and Joshua. Looking at her mother and sister, seeing broad smiles on their faces, she asked, "Were you two in on this?" She could see the guilty looks on their faces. "His girlfriend isn't going to be too happy about your matchmaking attempts." Although she was a bit peeved with her family members, she couldn't help but stare at this new Joshua.

Joshua's mother then spoke. "This new girlfriend you are talking about is his ex-wife, and she is remarried, so you don't need to worry about her. Also, after seeing you with Officer Duncan at your restaurant holding your hand the other day, he had given up hope on you because he thought you two were dating. But now, all the barriers to the two of you getting together have been removed."

Seeing the smug looks on everyone's faces, Marcie turned and walked over to her brother. "Were you in on this, too, brother?"

"I cannot tell a lie. Absolutely. I wouldn't miss out on this and let sis and mom have all the fun."

Now, standing so close to Joshua, she could feel her heart skip a beat or two. A shiver ran down her spine as he took her hands in his. That spark, that connection she had felt before when she started to get to know him, had now grown into a crescendo.

****

"So, as I understand it, Marcie, you are not dating or involved with Officer Duncan. And you know that the woman you saw me with is my ex, who has remarried. So, do you think there is a chance we could get to know each other a bit better?"

The smile on Marcie's face widened from ear to ear as she listened to me. Then, she couldn't hold back anymore. Reaching up with both hands, she took my face in her hands, pulled me closer, and kissed me as passionately as anyone had ever kissed me, including my ex-spouse.

Pulling away from me, she could now hear everyone in the restaurant clapping and cheering for them. She guessed she was making the right choice. And the look on my face told her she had.

J. A. Guinn

The End

ABOUT THE AUTHOR

Jon Guinn, a retired U.S. Air Force Lieutenant Colonel and Vietnam veteran, was born and raised in Walla Walla, Washington. He attended Washington State University, paying his way by working as a wildland firefighter and lookout for the U.S. Forest Service. After earning a degree in Police Science and Administration, he was commissioned as a second lieutenant in the Air Force Office of Special Investigations (AFOSI). During his time in the Air Force, he was selected to attend Turkish language school and was later assigned to Istanbul, Turkey, where he served as the detachment commander for AFOSI. While in Turkey, he developed an interest in writing after a dream that sparked a compelling spy storyline. Not having experience or even a natural talent for writing, he initially dismissed his interest; however, the intriguing plot kept haunting him, and he eventually gave in to his desire to try writing. He began working on his spy mystery manuscript on a small, portable typewriter in Istanbul in 1979. Unfortunately, that manuscript has been sitting in a drawer ever since.

After retiring from twenty years of service with the Air Force, Jon still felt a need to serve his local community. He trained as a volunteer firefighter and EMT at his local fire district. After ten rewarding years, he shifted to the Kootenai County Sheriff's Department as a background investigator and polygraph examiner. Upon full retirement, haunted by numerous firefighting incidents, the urge to write returned. That's when he began his first book, **Brotherhood of**

Fire. The excitement of publishing that book sparked ideas for sequels, leading **to Death Stalks the Fire Line.** The series concluded with **A Brother Down**. Someday, his original spy mystery set in Turkey may also come to life. His next book, **Valor in the Darkness** is just a wild idea that came to mind. I honor and respect all veterans; those with injuries and mental health issues still have much to offer our communities.